WEI TO GO!

WEI TO GO!

AN ELLIE & CO BOOK

LEE Y. MIAO

Summary: "Twelve-year-old Ellie, a third-generation Asian
American, journeys to Hong Kong and struggles to prevent a
mysterious corporation from jeopardizing her dad's California
firm and their family life."

&MG - An Imprint of Clear Fork Publishing

P.O. Box 870 102 S. Swenson

Stamford, Texas 79553 (915) 209-0003

www.clearforkpublishing.com

Printed in the United States of America

Softcover ISBN - 978-1-950169-67-2

I send love to my family who supports me in everything.

HONG KONG

Kowloon

Victoria Harbour

Star Ferry Pier

Guesthouse

Victoria Peak

Hong Kong
Island

Aberdeen

Stanley
Market

Ellie W. Pettit

Kowloon

1. History Museum
2. Intercontinental HK Hotel
3. Star Ferry Pier
4. YMCA
5. Peninsula Hotel
6. and 7. MTR exits

Nathan Road

Chatham Road S.

Salisbury Road

Victoria Harbour

Ellie W. Pettit

1

KINDA CLUELESS

I WANT to be totally alone. You could say I like taking my time to figure things out.

So I look around the kitchen to make sure. No wacky little brother and his loyal dog. And no snoopy—love 'em so much—parents.

I turn on the family computer to check out my swing before softball practice. Privately.

Now for my set-up. I straighten my GOOD GIRLS STEAL jersey. Pump up my skinny shoulders. Rearrange my ridiculously narrow feet. Raise my arms for the swing. Maybe they shouldn't be so high 'cause my hair falls and tickles my eyelashes.

Stop. Overthinking. Everything. Ellie. Yeah, I wish.

On the screen, the instructor takes forever with

an introduction, so I say, "Quit it and get on with the batting tips." It's only a video, so she never minds my sass.

A ball comes right toward me, spinning and hurtling. When it hunts me down, I swing with all my might. How did I do? I think I missed. Again.

That's when an open web page peeks out from the corner of the screen. I'm tempted.

Just so you know, I'm the only twelve-year-old with insane limits on screen time. Mom says I'm a sucker for clickbait whenever she warns, "Ellie, don't open things that are none of your business."

I pretend to turn up my nose. After a second, the corner of my eye veers toward it. I'll sorta click on the page, but not all the way. Nope, I won't. I can't help it if the web page baits my mouse—not me—to pounce.

I roll my eyes. I have no interest in Dad-stuff about some international business across the Pacific. He doesn't use the kitchen computer for his work, but he is a secret muncher. Fresh trails of orange cheese puffs by the keypad don't lie.

"El, water quick!" My brother Kipp rushes in with flashing dimples that let him get away with a lot, really a lot. Trotting right by him is Frankie, our part terrier, whose real name is Francesca.

She's so not into me.

"Frankie sure looks thirsty, too." I fill a water bowl, expecting no thanks from them.

Kipp attacks the faucet and chugs down his water, spilling it everywhere. Seeing my softball jersey, he shouts, "Ellie hammers the ball to the outfield and over the fence. See ya!"

If only. I hate it when he pretends to be a ball-park announcer. In a brotherly way.

I scrunch up my nose. "Are you cheering or trying to make fun of me?" No answer. I'm supposed to make us a snack, so I slap roasted turkey slices for two sandwiches and squirt buckets of mustard on mine. "Were you messing on the computer today at all?"

"N.O." He grabs his sandwich as I take a hurried bite on mine. Some mustard blobs spill, and I grab a sponge to wipe them up.

In a flash, Kipp grabs cheap wooden chopsticks Mom makes him use to eat slower. And scoops up the mustard blobs like they're ground balls in a lacrosse game. He flicks his wrist and says, "Sweet, watch this. I'm aiming for the sink."

Sink, my eye. Soggy, yellow darts splatter all over me.

I wave both hands in the air like I always do

when he ticks me off. In a sisterly way. "Now look at what you did—I have no clean jerseys. And I can't be late for practice."

Kipp lays down the chopsticks and wipes both hands on his food-stained T-shirt you can snack off. "My bad. What difference does it make? You get lost going anywhere."

"Trying to sell me a GPS?"

He grins and ignores that. "How many hits ya gonna get at practice?"

I'm ready. My mouth is crammed with whole wheat bread, so I fake my best big-sister smile and whip out an index card from my pocket to hand him.

Kipp wrinkles his nose and reads aloud what I copied from my *Little Brothers for Dummies* manual. "Someone forgot to tell you that you're not my coach. Now, get lost."

Surprise, surprise—he leashes Frankie and runs out after putting on his cap backward like he always does. "I'm walking her down to Wynnie's house."

That's so not possible. I peek out the living room window to see that I'm right. Frankie's yanking him down my favorite street where we're finally settled in a neighborhood outside of Los Angeles. I've got friends, a great school, and a softball team I love.

Like I never, ever want to leave my home here.

I grab a headband from my sports bag to pull back my messy brown hair. The attached name tag has a cuddly sea creature design. Right next to it are big letters shouting out my name, ELIZABETH W. PETTIT.

The *W* stands for a funny-looking Chinese name Wei (sounds like *way*). I don't know much about it. Kipp's got the same one, the only thing we have in common. He'd drool if a lacrosse coach yells, "Take it away, Wei!"

Not me. Sometimes I'm curious about my middle name, and other times I totally forget I have one. "Take it away, Pettit" sounds kinda off.

So I'm rushing out with my bag when the kitchen phone rings, but by the time I get to it, the answering machine kicks in. I stop to listen in case it's about practice.

A woman's voice tells someone in the background, "When I got wind of this a week ago, I never dreamed that—wait, I'll leave a message." She sounds worked up, but it's hard to tell without seeing her face. "Hello, hello? Is this Ken Pettit's home? I'm the company attorney. Ken, I couldn't reach you earlier, and something came up—"

I grab the phone. "Hi, I'm his daughter. May I help you?"

"Oh, thank you. Is your dad there? I couldn't reach him on his cell." She sorta sounds like she ran a mile uphill and stopped to breathe.

"He might be at the YMCA working out if he's turned off his phone. I could take a message." But if she does leave one, I'll be late. Coach Jen hates it when players don't arrive before practice starts. I have a special problem with that.

But I gotta be polite.

"Great—here's a temporary phone number. Tell him to call me ASAP," she says, sounding like a drama queen.

I learned once that ASAP means something important. "Can I tell him what it's about?"

"No, it's only a business matter. You won't forget my message, right?" Her voice softens and slows down before she hangs up. "Don't worry."

I write a quick note to Dad and paste it on the phone. Until I start thinking about why she would end the call with those *DW* words. It's probably nothing.

Sometimes parents like keeping things private until they can surprise you. Dad could have just landed another big customer. When we moved here, he started his own design company—that was a biggie for our family.

Other times, parents want to reassure you. Like the time I got on my first real bike and was afraid of falling off. Dad said, "Don't worry, I've got you." Or, right before I started a new school and thought I wouldn't make any friends, Mom said, "Don't worry, you definitely will."

Every once in a while, grown-ups want to protect you and pretend that everything's fine. Then they'll worry their heads off while forcing a smile. Nahh, too much thinking.

Like I said, it's probably nothing.

2

WAY TO GO

MOST KIDS DON'T THINK about being late. I do.

Kipp's right—I often do get lost. To make up for it, I figure I should be early when I can.

Today I'm gonna be on time, following two teammates on their bike as fast as possible. As we near the new practice field, I pass houses that all look alike. But straight up ahead is the perfect softball diamond—I never need a map to run the bases. That's if I get a hit.

The rest of the team is already here, including Cat (never Caterina). You won't believe what an awesome friend she is. Last year, we were assigned lockers near each other. When we slammed them both shut at the exact same time, we giggled and shrieked our heads off. I knew it was a sign from the locker gods to become besties right then and there.

"Missed you last time. Still stretching your leg?" I trade fist bumps with her and pick off a piece of lint from her jersey. She hurt herself in gym class a while ago.

"Yup. I'm thinking my arms will get me through the season." Cat swings her shoulders as her blonde ringlets poke out from under her cap.

"Aw, you always get on base—you're the best player." I'm not just saying that. She really is amazing in both hitting and defensive plays.

"Yeah, but you're the fastest runner. By the way, I'm going out of town for a few days. Wanna get together when I return?"

"OK, can't wait. Um, you said your dad works in a law office. Does he ever make work calls on weekends?"

"Only if it's urgent." Cat scans my face and right away, she adds, "Why?"

"Right before I left the house, dad's company lawyer called. She got all weird and then pretended everything was normal." I shake my head.

"Who knows what grown-ups mean half the time? Sometimes my dad gets all hyped up about some phrase in a contract. Can you believe it?" She giggles.

I giggle back. "Yeah, my dad is like that, too. After practice, I'll hurry back and see if he's home. Oops, we're starting." Cat and I join our other teammates to stretch and do drills.

After an hour, we're about finishing up and I'm ready to take off my cleats. I want to be the first one out of here.

Coach Jen gathers the team around her. "Listen up. We'll go over one extra batting strategy to focus on fundamentals." She plays on the high school team and says what's good for them is good for us Stealers, too. "Ask yourself three things before stepping up to the batter's box."

One, what do I want to do with the ball—hit it near or far?

Two, where do I want to hit it—in the air or on the ground?

Three, how far do I want to go—single, double, or home run?

"Also, in a real game, don't stand there watching where the ball goes. Close the deal and run." Coach looks around before staring at me. "Now who wants to step up and help demonstrate?"

Last year I was a newbie and hardly ever got a

hit. This summer I don't have one good excuse. Everyone knows it.

I'm telling you, it's hard to stay invisible. I slide my hand over the yellow mustard streaks on my jersey. But science class teaches every action has an equal and opposite reaction.

I forgot.

Coach sees my hand and marches toward me like I'm caught giving signals to the other team. She towers over me while handing me a bat. It's true what Dad always says—the cover-up is what gets you.

"Me?" I take the bat and put it down. First, I clap off my hands still caked with disgusting dugout dirt. And take my time latching my helmet. I'm not going to choke.

First pitch. Choke—my setup was insane.

Second pitch. Choke—the pitch came at a stinking speed.

Third pitch. Choke—my back leg itched like crazy when I shifted my weight.

Coach Jen calls out, "Next."

I shrug and plod away from the batter's box but suddenly pivot. "Since this is practice, how about one more swing? Please?"

"Really? OK, OK, do-over." She tries hard not to

smile. That's nice of her since high school girls are always in a hurry.

The fourth pitch is when my video's slump-busting tips kick in. I can't complain when the ball cracks the sweet spot—without me analyzing or overthinking. Boy, do I feel good about my ball drilling straight to the outfield.

Cat cheers as she and my Stealers team crowd around like they always do, even when I flub up, and wave their wristbands. Now about those little round rubber pieces—they're special 'cause a player only gets one after scoring a run for the first time. I'm dying to get one but haven't earned one. Yet.

"Way to go—this is your year, Ellie," shouts Coach Jen with her thumbs up. She faces the team and says, "Bring it in, guys. Now, if I'm busy at practices, check out the right experts for help." She points to the parent volunteers, waving at us to show how much they want to help with batting and fielding. "See you next time and don't be late."

Yeah, if I can get home from today's session. On my way here, it was easy following two bikes. But I need to leave now. Alone.

"See ya," I yell out and bike away from the field.

———

TOWARD HOME CAN BE TOUGH. Outside the softball diamond, I'm kinda challenged with directions. I often can't get straight to my house, and I don't think about it until I can't.

Grown-ups say insane things like "No one gets lost with a cell phone." Hahahahaha. Even with a cell, sometimes I can't form what Mom calls a mental map that will take me places.

It's like insisting spelling rookies use a dictionary. They're not going to win the spelling bee the next day. Or the next. Or the next, next, and next.

My hand-me-down cell from Mom is so ancient that it doesn't even have GPS. It doesn't matter because in my neighborhood, my parents want me to practice with landmarks.

After I take the short walkway bridge over a dry creek and leave the bike path, I go back and forth and stop. And tell myself not to panic. At least it's never muggy—the kind that feels like worms are crawling under my skin. The Los Angeles area has dry-as-toast weather I love.

When a woman with a floppy gardening hat appears in her yard, I exhale. "Hi, I'm a little lost—can you help me?" I tell her my street name.

"No problem, it's really close. Here's what you do."

After every street she mentions, I nod and repeat, "Uh huh, uh huh" when I'm kinda clueless. She smiles when I agree with everything. I'm happy that she's happy.

Before walking to her front door, she says, "You can't miss it."

Groan. I hate when someone says that.

Ten minutes later, it's like I've been circling for an hour. When my wheels pass a crooked tree trunk I recognize, I finally arrive on my street.

Woo-hoo!

I dash into my house where mudroom perfume slams my nostrils. Lacrosse gloves and sticks and soccer balls—whatever—all smell nasty like week-old sweat. Pinching my nose, I place my glove and bat in the cleanest corner. No way I'll be a two-sport-plus jock like Kipp.

In the hallway across from the kitchen, a tall shadow is bent out of shape against a sunshiny patch of light. "You think this BT Group will get away with the takeover? My family always comes first." Dad perks up when he sees me and ends the call, murmuring, "Talk later."

I walk up and tug the arm of my best buddy. "Hey, I heard you say *family*. Are you talking with that lawyer who called? What about?"

Dad pats my head while fidgeting with the pencil in his shirt pocket. He tries to keep his voice calm, and that makes me kinda suspicious. "It's a work matter. We might have some changes, that sort of thing."

"But you only started your company about a year ago. What kind of changes?" I remember the weird web page on the kitchen computer about some business in Asia.

"At times a firm wants to expand its activities." He plows his hands through messy blondish hair, something I usually don't see him do.

"So, your company will get into other art and designs? That's great, Dad." Whew, what a relief.

"Not quite, but I don't have all the details. Don't worry."

I wish he hadn't said that.

Before he trudges down the hall, he hugs me so quickly I feel cheated. "And don't go asking your mom." That's so freaking scary because lots of times he'll say, "Go ask your mom." Well, except on Mother's Day.

Here's the thing. I love my little brother and my mom. They're the best.

But I'm really tight with my dad, and I'd do

anything for him. Of course, he'd usually tell me things aren't what they seem.

I do a Google search on the kitchen computer for help. On his cell, Dad said something about a takeover, whatever that is. The Internet tells me why one company would take over another.

One, to grab another company's product that's not making money.

Two, to get into different products.

Three, to knock out competition for the same product.

All of this literally makes no sense.

When I hear footsteps coming my way, I log out and turn around so fast my foot bumps against the trash can and the contents spill out. A torn piece of paper with the words *Kong* and *itinerary* stick out at the top, which I pull out and crush in my pocket.

Mom comes in all quiet, not joking as she usually does in the kitchen. All her meals end in a *dinggg* because for her, *cook* is a four-letter word. She usually orders healthy takeout food and nukes it. Except on Friday nights when she orders pizza with her stash of coupons.

And she's happy as long as Dad's cholesterol "is below 200 and his waist size stays below X-large."

"Why are you here?" I ask.

"I live here."

"Where's Dad?"

She gasps a little and ties back her ruffled hair before plastering on a flimsy smiley face. "Oh, he ran off to the office."

"On a Saturday—what for?"

Mom ignores me and marches toward the pantry. "I'm making an early dinner."

Is she upset? You could say that.

It's another punch to my gut.

3

A WRINKLE

I'LL BET Dad told her something. He's thinking about that business thing, and that means Mom's worrying that he's worrying. I don't know if I should be worried, too.

Kipp and Frankie come into the kitchen. She growls and tilts her head with blackish hair that almost covers her eyes and hot pink collar. I try to pull her toward me, but she does a U-ey and jumps into his waiting arms.

Traitor. I don't spoil her with lots of treats, but she's supposed to be my dog, too. "Kipp, can you hold her? She thinks a stranger is in the pantry. And Mo-om, aren't we having takeout today?"

There's always an exception. She comes out with her items, shakes her head, and heads toward the stove like a chef ready to make a gourmet meal. Her one and only masterpiece is Spanish Rice.

A little while later, I face leftover pasta sauce smothered over nervous grains of larvae-looking pellets. I guess that's dinner tonight.

Kipp and I take a few bites, holding our breaths from the smell of chalk-dry, burnt rice.

Chef Mom threw out the rice cooker Dad got for her birthday a long time ago.

"Something's kicking up Kipp's allergies. And I'm full—we'll finish up later." To him, I whisper, "You're *wel*come."

Mom rises from the scratched-up butcher block table and peers at him. Without a word, she places the leftover larvae in baggies to join last year's supply in the freezer. Afterward, she straightens the "Eat at Your Own Risk" sign someone slapped on the fridge. Normally she'd grumble and say "smart alecks" while trying to hide her giggles.

Normally.

Kipp's new T-shirt of the day says TO BE NO. 1, TRAIN LIKE YOU'RE NO. 2. He tries this out with a tug-of-rope toy on Frankie. "Who's a good girl? Are you a good girl? Go fetch."

I need to get back on the computer. It's not easy being alone in the kitchen where I share the family computer. "Guys, I want to get a head start on some summer homework that's been posted. I can't stand being interrupted *ad nauseam*." This Latin word that means *sickening* comes in so handy.

"Always a word nerd." Kipp sticks out his tongue at me.

Mom steps in. "I wish you wouldn't call Ellie that. Try something more positive like *word enthusiast*."

"Excuse me, but I happen to know he won't use four syllables when one will do." I roll my eyes. "And guess what? Ms. Ohara will be my English teacher again. So, I could use some peace and quiet to look at her reading list."

"Wonderful—I'll leave you alone. I'll pay bills and do other paperwork."

"Speaking of paper, uh, weren't you supposed to go soon on that conference trip you won? Your itinerary was in the trash can all ripped up," I say.

"Your dad's company has lots going on, so I'm going to stick around." Mom smiles.

"But you said you really wanted to go. And you were planning to visit a friend there."

She walks out, saying, "Well, I guess that won't happen now. It's all good."

That's not what I'd call a legit answer.

Now that Mom's gone, Kipp quickly nukes our go-to lifesavers—turkey hot dogs and buns—and gives Frankie her usual cut for alerting us to the stranger in the pantry. We gobble down our food and smack our lips.

I need to work. He and our dog have got to leave. "Wouldn't she love a pawsome pit stop?"

We hear a noise off the kitchen, and Kipp says, "Wait, that's for me." He opens the back door where whispers about something *GF* takes place.

Our neighbor Wynnie comes in, brown bangs combed neatly, and looks at me shyly the way I look up at high school girls. "Hey, Ellie."

"That necklace is adorbs. Where are you hanging out these days?"

"Thanks, I'm crazy about beads—I made it at a crafts workshop. I'm gonna start the Y math camp with a new counselor. Numbers are *sooo* cool." She blushes and adjusts her glasses.

"You'll cover those cute angles that drove me crazy." I snicker.

Kipp leashes Frankie. "Uh, Wynnie's going to show me her soccer trophies."

"Don't forget to call if you'll be late," shouts out a voice from the hallway. She's got hyper-excellent hearing, our mom.

"I would if I had my own cell," he whines, shouting back. He's so rubbing it in.

Before school starts, I'll get a new cell for taking a Chinese heritage class that meets one last time. "Get over it, Kipp. I earned it by working my behind off, and you'll have to take the next session. I'm the guinea pig for classes and camps, remember?"

Wynnie waves bye as Kipp says, "No way for Wei. And gee, I don't remember you getting into sports first. See ya."

It's true—I don't pick up sports as easily as him. Guinea pigs have it tough sometimes. Even heritage class was tough.

I don't know what it means to be part Chinese. Mom might look Chinese, but she's totally American. I'm me, whatever that is. Sometimes I know I'm special. Most of the time I'm mixed up about it. She bribed me to sign up for the class.

Like that's supposed to help me figure out who I am.

The mother of the bribe pokes her head into the kitchen. Startled, I blurt out, "Is Dad back?"

"Not yet. Listen, your heritage teacher left a confusing message about canceling your last class."

I pump my fist in the air. "Yay—let the summer begin. What did it say?"

"Something like *lose a horse, gain two*. Did you learn that curious phrase in class?"

"Maybe it means canceling can be something good. Mr. Han recited these Chinese expressions while the class guessed what the heck he meant. He drove us nuts when he did that."

After Mom's gone, I end up snoozing in my room with the door ajar. It's weird, but the sound of hushed-up voices wakes me up.

Dad's voice whispers shrilly, "Say nothing to the kids yet."

The last time I heard them whispering was when they surprised us with Frankie joining our family. Before that he and Mom were acting secretive about money and budgets when our ancient bathroom pipes had to be ripped up.

So I don't know if it's something good. Or something bad that's expensive.

Tiptoeing into the family room, I dive behind an armchair. From there, I can peek at the patio through the screen door.

I triple swear on my hardback copy of *A Wrinkle in Time* that I'm not snooping.

Mom plasters a hand to her mouth. "So what'd the company attorney say?"

"She confirmed the business acquisition by this

BT Group." Dad paces back and forth with a bag of cheese puffs. "I'm to place all of Avabrand's new designs on hold indefinitely."

"What's this BT Group after? Your company was doing so well after launching the sea animal series." She sighs and shakes her head. "And what does this mean for you?"

"I have no idea why a private Hong Kong corporation wants this takeover out of the blue. It'll force Avabrand to fold, and we'll have to move if I can't find a job here."

"After we finally settled in this terrific place. If you need to go job-hunting, we'll dip into our savings." Mom drops the worn cushion cover she's mending and grabs Dad's hands. "I'm worried that Ellie won't forgive us. Hopefully, moving is a worst-case scenario."

Move. Not again. It stinks to be the new girl. Triple moves since kindergarten. At the last place, we didn't even unpack all our stuff. I used to think if only Dad had his own company, life would be perfect. Now this.

He always explained if something happens to his company, he'd have to start all over. He works on special designs and finding the right people to work with him could take forever.

"I've got to slip back out. Things are happening even as we speak." Dad rubs Mom's cheek with his fingers like he always does when she's upset.

A furry creature comes up and sniffs all over me. I whisper-screech softly, "Frankie, bad timing." The sniffing continues. So much for her English. I try some Chinese, but—oops—Mom never bribed her. She trots away, and I hear a crash-landing sound in the kitchen.

"Wait, what was that? Let me check." Mom says bye to Dad and collects her stuff. She's about ready to approach the screen door, and that means afterward, she'll have to pass me.

This is when P.E. class comes in handy like you wouldn't believe. Pulling my head back, I crouch even lower to do bear crawls, the ones I used to hate, from furniture to furniture. Once in the kitchen, I dash out of the house and walk down the street.

If we move again, Cat won't be my bestie. I'll have to start with new streets and landmarks so I won't lose my way. It'll take forever to call a new house my home. A nightmare.

Kipp won't make it to fifth grade here with Wynnie and all his sports buddies. I won't see my softball team and other friends again. I'll never get a wristband for my first run.

Talk about life sticking it to us.

Bluish-purplish jacaranda trees on my street finished their knockout run. Who knows if I'll ever see them again when they bloom next spring? I end up a block away at my favorite little park to sit and think. From my deep pocket, I pull out a little black journal and pencil.

When my English teacher Ms. Ohara isn't giving us reading lists, she emphasizes the power of the pen for ideas. To her, a goal without a plan is just a wish.

Think, Ellie, think. I could sure use a chocolate bar to help me. But I don't have one.

So, I come up with a strategy like what Coach Jen told my Stealers team.

One, what do I want to do—help Dad.

Two, how do I do that—

- Look up company takeovers – Done, sort of.
- Get info on BT Group.
- Beg BT Group to stop taking over Dad's company.

Three, how far do I want to go—won't rest until his company is safe.

There.

Spotting a stray lacrosse ball, I get up to pick it up for Kipp.

Someone beats me to it. Today of all days, out of nowhere.

He's a guy from my homeroom who's also in my math class. I'm going to play it cool and grin, and I don't care if he'll see a parade of silvery turquoise tinsel on my teeth.

I do not have a crush on him. Period.

But I wouldn't mind getting to know him better. "Hey, Russ." My voice comes out a little squeaky.

"S'up? What are you doing this summer?" Sparkling eyes like you wouldn't believe peer out from under his cap.

"Um, I've got lots of softball practice and other stuff." O.M.G. That came out so wrong.

"Oh, so you're busy." He scoops up the ball and lobs it to me, mumbling, "Here you go."

Just because I play softball doesn't mean I can catch anything from only three feet away. I kneel down to pick it up as my headband takes a dive. And yank up the blindfold.

He's gone. I practically shouted I was swamped and couldn't talk.

Why then would he ever want to hang out.

4

HELP WANTED

FREAKING T-SHIRTS. You've got to focus, Ellie. And think about him another time.

Back home, I pass the living room couch. Ages ago in another house, my family watched a movie about a sassy guinea pig singing in a flash mob dance. I got up to sing the same song and dropped my juice pack. As I started crying, Dad picked me up and sang made-up words for me. Boy, does he have an awful voice, but I loved it. Afterward, he hugged me and gently set me on that couch.

He helped me, and now I've got to help him.

Everyone says I inherited Dad's nose but got skipped for his blue eyes and drawing skills. But they're overrated. I've got his smile but nothing to smile about now.

In the kitchen, I look up the BT Group. The website is practically blank—like where are the funny-looking skyscrapers and rows of look-alike windows I wouldn't want to clean. Nowhere do I see smiling workers with zit-free skin not wearing braces. A plain page asks for a username and password. It's one of those private websites. A dead end.

I have no idea who can help me get information, and I don't know anyone from Asia.

That's when I remember Coach Jen saying, "Check out the right experts for help." Out comes my little black journal again.

Dad—want to help him secretly

Mom—can't worry her

Ms. Ohara—school's out

Coach Jen—softball season

Cat—out of town

Russ—I'd rather die

Kipp—kiss of death

No one. N.O.

Wait—except Mr. Han. He grew up in northern China but told the class he lives in Hong Kong now, except in the spring. That's when he comes over and teaches my heritage class here.

I storm down the hallway. "Mom-Mom, did Mr. Han give an email or something in his message canceling the last class?"

"Honey, slow down. No, it was an automated call. Why?"

"You're kidding, right?" I howl like Frankie when she hears a siren.

Mom puts her hand to her ear. "Should I get my hearing checked? Before taking the class, your exact words were 'Ten afternoons after school? Make me.' But—"

"I was a little snarky to him at first. He pronounced my last name *petite* instead of Pettit."

"Ah, Elizabeth, a middle name perhaps?" Mr. Han had asked me on my first day. Another girl with the same first name was in our class.

"Yeah," I said and opened my lesson book.

"What is it, if you don't mind my asking?"

"It's my mom's last name, W-e-i." I turned to the next page.

"Ah. Wei, Wei, Wei," he said to me.

Why, why, why. "Um, would you mind calling me Elizabeth P.?"

He's called me that ever since. And now he's gone.

I snort in disgust. "Why did he have to cancel the last class?"

"If I could finish," says Mom. "The message said tomorrow he'll hold a short wrap-up instead. I didn't think you'd be interested."

———

I LIKE RIDING shotgun with Dad. Especially since Kipp's too young to do that. Today (and only today) I wish like heck he's with us. Usually Dad and I talk nonstop, but he's totally quiet.

In the next five minutes, the car makes a crunching sound, right during rush-hour traffic on the freeway. Dad does a slow roll over to the shoulder and fidgets with some gizmo.

"Hurry, hurry—I can't miss the class wrap-up. What if it's over when I arrive?" I stick out my tongue at the rubbernecking cars. "We could ask the police to escort me with sirens."

He chuckles, his slow one that goes on and on. "Before your first class, I had to unlatch your hands and feet from the windshield and practically push you in."

"Sheesh, that was in the beginning. You keep forgetting that afterward, I got to really like the class and Mr. Han." About a century later, we're on our way. "Uh, you've still got that new plastic strip stuck down your pant leg."

Dad laughs and rips it off. "Hey, my new pants size is top-secret info."

"I didn't peek at the number. If I did accidentally, I won't tell Mom—she's obsessed about your cholesterol thing." I get ready to ask my first business question. "By the way, the Internet says companies have to make money. So is your yours, um, doing OK?"

His eyebrows do funny question marks as he glances at me. "You're too young to know how business works. But anyhow, we're profitable with some outside investors."

So, his company's making money. That means it can't be reason number one on my list about takeovers. "Whatever. Here's a real dumb one. How do you get your ideas?"

"No such thing as a dumb question. Many times it's out of the blue. I could have seen or read something, and years later it'll materialize. That's why I carry an old-fashioned sketch pad all the time." He pulls up to the building. "Have a good class, Sport."

"You rock, Dad."

"Booyah."

"Uh, booyah to you, too. Love ya." I can't make

fun of his cute kid-talk from yesterday. He's so brave about not letting on about his work problems.

Walking through the classroom door, I avoid the kid who teased me during my first class. He said some rotten things while pointing to his inky black hair and eyes that aren't the same as mine. Like "Hey, your hair's not jet-black, and you're half and half."

I remember gritting my teeth and stammering, "I'm not a coffee creamer."

"Does it matter? Half and half make a whole," Mr. Han interrupted us while passing out the lesson material. He sure knew how to shut down what that kid said.

Just because someone looks different doesn't mean it's bad.

I almost quit after a few classes, but Mr. Han is the easiest teacher to talk to. He always tells me, "You fit right in, Elizabeth P."

He even became the homework helper to a bunch of us kids. That's 'cause some parents, like Mom, couldn't tell my written characters looked like baby carrots on crutches.

One tiny stroke makes a Chinese character different from another with a totally different meaning. It's like adding an apostrophe to my English teacher's name, Ms. Ohara. Her family name, from

Japan, might turn into an Irish one like Scarlett O'Hara.

Mr. Han whooshes in and walks past my desk. I tug on his elbow and ask to see him later, but he says he's in a rush. A zillion worry stripes must have been dancing on my face, so he changes his mind.

After class, he hurriedly puts on a light jacket over his cricket shirt. When I first moved here, I was surprised many June evenings in Southern California are cool and gloomy. But I'm on to him about sports clothing. We bonded over his stories about playing cricket in Hong Kong and baseball here.

"Ah, Elizabeth P., how's everything?"

I twiddle with my headband. "My dad's the art director of this company Avabrand he started. He works mostly on tiny sea animal designs, like starfish and seahorses. They're plastered on clothes and sports bags."

"What's the problem?" Mr. Han yawns, reminding me of Granddad who passed away a while ago. "Sorry, I've become a night owl. Instead of staying up, I should exercise more."

"The company's small but making waves. But get this—some big, weird Hong Kong company called the BT Group wants to take over his company. It's so ridiculous."

Mr. Han clamps his mouth shut as his eyes grow big. While scratching his blackish-grayish hair, his baseball cap falls off. "I'm so sorry to hear that."

I pick up his cap with a black nautical symbol on the front. Could be a turtle. "Didn't you say your other job is in Hong Kong? I can't find any info on this BT company—the website asks for a username and password. And I've got to help Dad like now."

"What'd you have in mind?"

"I might use social media to beg some executives to leave Avabrand alone. My parents don't know that I know. And I can't screw up."

"Kids are supposed to screw up. Social media might be ineffective in this case—the Black Turtle Group is an intensely private company."

"Black Turtle Group? Oh—BTG. Well, so much for that idea."

Mr. Han checks his watch. "You once mentioned playing softball. My idol, a pitcher named Walter Johnson, stressed you can't hit what you can't see. I'm thinking you should find a way to go and pitch your case. How would you feel about that?"

"All the way, like to Hong Kong? Well, my mom did win this contest for a conference there, but she's canceling." I pull back my hair and adjust my headband. "I could try, but nah, that's crazy. Plus, long plane rides make me puke. I hate getting all nauseous."

"Imagine two teams tied at the bottom of the final inning. You're the next batter—what will you do?"

"Scream help?"

"Ah, Elizabeth P., take risks to get rewards. No dawdling and no overthinking as some corporate decisions are made fantastically fast," says Mr. Han. When his cell starts singing, he glances down at the number. "I need to take this."

After a minute, his shoulders tense up. "You say 280—an unbelievable price to pay in any situation. Is she available the next few days? I'll be traveling shortly, so I'll call back in a second."

Freaking T-shirts. One second to decide.

5

GOTTA SWING

"ARE YOU ALL RIGHT, Mr. Han? You look kinda spooked."

He sighs, shoving his lesson material into a brief-case. "Something urgent came up, so I must go."

"Wait, I think . . . maybe . . . OK, I'm in. I'll beg Mom to not cancel her trip but won't tell her my secret plans," I say excitedly. "I'm sure she'll take me. At last, I'll have a vacation away from my annoying little brother."

Mr. Han nods and mutters something in a language that I don't understand.

I hesitate. "Can you help? It'd be great if I met some top executive man face to face."

"Ah, Elizabeth P., don't assume all executives are men. What would you say?"

My chin quivers, but I'm not crying. "I'll prepare a speech to say how hard Dad and his employees work and that they all have families. They're not only designers, they're also people."

"Excellent. I'm returning to Hong Kong myself, but first, I must deal with a personal and work-related matter. Once there, I'll be extraordinarily busy with new volunteer work." Mr. Han changes the tone of his voice like he's telling me a secret. "I do know some BTG management, so let me try reaching someone. The guy I know the best goes to the gym a lot, what I'm supposed to be doing."

"Wow—you know someone there?" Looking past him to the open door, Dad's car is pulling into the parking lot.

Mr. Han heads outside with me. "Yes, but it's always hectic when I return. Anyhow, when the student is ready, the teacher will appear. Ah, I appreciate this slightly cool LA evening. I hate the miserable heavy showers in Hong Kong." He scribbles something on a piece of paper and hands it to me. "Here are some places to visit or have a meeting when you're running around."

"Awesome, but what do you mean *running around*?"

"Ah, Elizabeth P., remember to keep your head above water."

"There's something else."

He interrupts gently. "I remember one of your recent homework mentioned you turned twelve. A black turtle, according to the water element."

"Finding my way in new—"

"It doesn't matter. When you commit to helping your dad, all sorts of things will occur that wouldn't have been possible. Take risks, take swings." He pulls out his cell. "Remember that family is the most important thing in life. And good things come to those who go."

"I—I guess so." I cram his note in my plaid backpack.

"Oops, I've got to take this international call." He rushes to his car, talking nonstop on his cell. Then he stops and shouts like he's gone bonkers. "He did what?"

Turning to me, he smiles with crinkly eyes and calls out, "Have fun, Elizabeth P."

———

I wish grown-ups would stop saying to have fun.

Nobody says that before I brush my teeth or eat

breakfast. But grown-ups shout it in your face before a sports game on the line or before a final exam. Now I've got to persuade my parent to go on a major trip and take me with her. To have fun.

Mom returns from an errand. After she parks her car on the street and walks up the short driveway, we meet halfway. She normally doesn't wear makeup, but a ton of blusher would help. "How was your wrap-up session, Ellie?"

"It was *sooo* good. Mr. Han told the class to practice the language as much as we can—starting now." I grab one of her bags and walk with her.

"That's great. Let me catch your dad." Her worry lines, what she calls them, are almost popping out of her forehead.

"Um, could you still go on your trip? Since Dad's busy, isn't it the perfect time to go? I mean, it's not like you win contests every day. And I could tag along."

My neighbor Abbey's screen door opens with a slight squeak.

"Tag along? Where's this coming from? For one thing, I'd be busy. Plus, we'd have to pay for your plane ticket."

"Would it be cheaper to go by boat, like a fast one?" I ask.

Mom starts to turn green. "No, a plane should do. Thank you very much."

Abbey, wearing a sun hat over her fluffy red hair, comes over and unlatches the fence gate. "Hey, softball player, we thought we heard you talking."

Her two little boys run out and grab my legs and arms while she talks to Mom. They crawl all over me like lovable puppies curious about everything and dying to cuddle and share. "Ellie, where's Frankie? We want to show you our new toy. When are you gonna babysit again?"

"Very soon—I can't wait." I swing hands and hug them before they start playing together. "Guess what, Abbey? I might be out of town for a little while. Mom might take me with her to Hong Kong."

"Lucky you—overseas trips are so educational. My boys will be so disappointed. Oh, look at the time." She calls out to them.

"They sure are close. When I babysat and they wanted the same toy, I separated them. But then they couldn't stand being apart."

Abbey laughs as she rounds up her family. "The connection between brothers can be so special. Do something fantastic in Hong Kong, and tell us all about it when you're back."

"Actually, nothing's been decided yet. Good to see you." Mom nudges me to the back door.

In the kitchen, I ask if she has lots of airline frequent flyer miles she always brags about.

She says, "I sure do, but I'd rather save them for a future flight."

"Isn't this the perfect time to cash in? And I'll bet you already canceled all your work stuff for the week."

Mom's eyes roam upward from one part of the ceiling to the other end. Finally, she says, "Even with your free ticket, we'd still have to buy one for your brother. Last-minute tickets are horrendously expensive."

I'm a big sister. I love my family. But I have my limits. "Kipp? Why does he have to go? He does the wackiest things with toilet paper. And all he does is talk sports when he's not carrying his lacrosse stick or walking Frankie. Couldn't Dad take him to the office a few times?"

"Hon, that's not a good idea. He's dealing with that emergency."

"If Kipp goes, you'd have to worry about two kids instead of one," I say.

"If you go, he goes."

Mom doesn't understand limits.

But I can't jeopardize her taking me. "Let's say, for fun, that he goes. Cat says her mom books these last-minute tickets all the time for her work trips. You'd think they'd cost a ton, but lots of times they're cheaper."

"Why don't you take a look? I'll talk with your dad about tentative plans."

Tentative? I won.

Sort of, if you call going with Kipp a win.

That evening Mom stands beside me with her credit card while showing me how to book the flights. I'm about to hit the enter key when Kipp runs in and yells "Sweet."

Except he bumps into me, forcing my pinkie to slam the delete key.

"Why'd you do that?" I want to yell, but not with Mom right by me. He escapes out of the kitchen while I type hyperfast to re-input all the info.

Best dad in the universe comes into the kitchen and acts normal. "Is the Kippster in the doghouse again? I had to detour around a huddled body in the hallway."

Take risks. Take swings.

I say, "Um, none of us have been to Hong Kong, and Mom will be busy. Can I take charge of what to do and where to go?"

Dad grins, nodding to Mom. "What? We'll shoot fireworks if you take charge."

"Is that a yes?" My cheeks are getting awfully warm.

"Come on, we're kidding," she says.

Except they're not. To them, I'm a "I have to think about this" or "it seems like it's kinda maybe OK" daughter.

"Take it easy and remember that trips can be very hectic. At times you won't get perfect information, so make do with what you've got," says Dad. "Otherwise, waffling might slow you down. Relax and don't be afraid to ask for help, either."

It doesn't help when parents say things that are so meh. "Whatever. The tickets haven't cleared yet 'cause the spinning beach ball is on the screen."

A second later, *bling*. Two tickets confirmed. I have no excuses.

I get up and shout out to the hallway. "Kipp—we're going!"

"Way ahead of you, Sister," he says, returning to the kitchen. "I got a friend to walk Frankie during the day, if anyone cares."

Dad ruffles Kipp's brown mop. "Thanks, and don't forget to behave. Keep that water handy." He turns to me. "Take it easy before you get into the swing of things in softball."

"Cute pun. I'll write down all my impressions." I hold up my small travel journal and give him the biggest hug ever. "I love you, Dad."

One family and two kids with one middle name. Three months before seventh grade, and I'm traveling across the Pacific to save my dad's company. With my little brother—ugh.

I'm not going to choke.

DAY ONE

6

GET OFF THE BOAT

"My butt hurts." A few days later on the plane, Kipp isn't afraid to tell us his personal problem.

"Behind," says a drowsy voice. It's true—Mom really can hear slang in her sleep.

"Behind what?" He grumbles about word nerds under his breath.

"Lose the word *butt* and stop picking your nose," I say.

"You butt out, El, and shut up."

"I heard that." Mom sits up and dictates, "Kipp, take a hike—go."

Sometimes she's kinda strict and asks me to stop being so sassy and mouthing off to Kipp.

I avoid her eyes to pick up a discarded cup and napkins. "He's messy as those baseball dugouts. He knows the trip takes about fourteen hours, so how can his behind hurt so soon?"

"How about cutting him some slack? He's a little nervous on his first long plane ride."

Mom sweeps back a dangling lock of my hair. "You don't need to boss him around so much."

"Why is it that I'm bossy, and you call him confident if he says the same thing?"

"Do I?" She turns redder than our neighbor Abbey's hair. "I'll be more careful. By the way, I'm glad you persuaded me to go. I can't wait to attend my Find-a-New-Hobby conference. It'll be good to step away from my day job." All week she helps people select personalized invitations. Thick cream-colored cotton paper announcing babies, weddings, bar mitzvahs, and all kinds of parties.

"But you're always drooling over elegant stationery."

Mom stretches and curls her fingers. "It's good to try something different, sort of like a mom-cation. I want to get my hands dirty." She leans back in her seat.

"Not me." I shudder and pretend to look at my summer reading list. I love reading but not off a list. Mom says I should, and Dad says keep reading whatever interests me. The "should" parent cocoons in her window seat with her dark brown mophead peeking up over her blanket.

Mr. Han mentioned water in his scribbled notes. Hong Kong's an archipelago. That's 260 islands. Sheesh. I don't know how I'm going to get anything done.

A place called Kowloon has a pier with ferry service. Aberdeen is another place with a harbor that's near the Stanley Market, a shopping hot spot. Everyone visits Victoria Peak, the highest point on Hong Kong Island where you get great views of the harbors and other islands.

With my headset on, I take a break and flip through the TV channels. Watching a movie or the weather report isn't my thing.

As I'm scrolling through, I yank up my head when a British Broadcasting Corporation (BBC) report flashes, "Business update—Black Turtle Group Takeover?"

A reporter announces, "This just in. Rumors are swirling about the fiercely competitive tycoon and CEO of the Black Turtle Group, the privately held conglomerate worth billions." She reads from her notes. "The company's takeover of a local Hong Kong business will be concluded soon. He is considering expansion of his design subsidiary with a first-time ever acquisition in the Los Angeles area. In other business news, the chairperson of the board of directors—"

The Los Angeles area. With trembling fingers, I snatch the black journal from my backpack and reread my notes on takeovers.

One, to grab another company's product that's not making money.

Two, to get into different products.

Three, to knock out competition for the same product.

I already know it's not reason one since Dad told me his company makes money. The news says the BT Group has some design company. To me, that means taking over Avabrand isn't getting into different products. So, it's also not reason number two.

That only leaves reason number three. What if BTG wants to knock out the competition with Dad's small firm to make lots more money? They both do designs, and maybe the bad guy will destroy Avabrand. I scribble in some question marks and underline it. Like I really know what any of this means.

Cat and I once saw a movie about Wall Street men with fancy laptops in dark offices, secretly taking over mom-and-pop shops. They wore razor-sharp jackets and ties with tiny hatchet designs. Killer hanky triangles peeked out of their crooked suit pockets. These were men without families who wrecked small firms after looking at phony reports with lots of lying math.

I clutch my tummy and turn to Mom who's tugging her blanket and stretching her neck. "Um, I wasn't snooping, but I overheard you and Dad talking about Avabrand. Is that Hong Kong company really going to take it over?"

She sits up, hugging her pillow. "Your dad's trying to figure things out with very limited information. As a toddler, you were scared to go down our back patio step, but your grandparents told you not to fear the unknown."

"What if we have to move for him to start up again? I can't ever leave my friends and our neighborhood. Aren't you scared?"

"You can't scare me—I have kids. Anyhow, things aren't carved in stone yet. Sometimes things work out, so stop worrying and have fun."

Have fun? I have things to do and places to go. "When are we arriving?"

"Can you look for the tickets in my tote? I'm hoping it won't take long to get to the guesthouse. I want to call your dad before he leaves for work—there's that time difference."

I read off our airline tickets. "It's Saturday now, and we'll get in Sunday night about 8 o'clock." I jerk up from my seat. "Only five days in Hong Kong? I forgot we'll lose a day after crossing that International Date Line thing."

"Who's having a date?" asks Kipp, plopping down on his seat.

"Was I talking romance? You need an atlas. Didn't you cover that imaginary vertical line in the Pacific, the zig-zaggy one?"

"What's that got to do with play dates?"

"My bad, you're not in fifth grade yet." I sigh.

"So when we leave Hong Kong on Friday, it'll still be Friday when we're back home. Tomorrow will be today." He always nails those things, Kipp does.

"Sheesh, that means we'll lose Friday, too. Oh, and you've got toilet paper stuck to your sneaker." I'm telling you, he doesn't nail everything.

Finding out I've got four days to get anything done is a rotten way to start the trip.

"TP can be clean, you know." Kipp jerks the arm rest down like a border wall between us and points upward. "Hey El, watch and learn when I touch the light bulb icon on my screen."

"So, you're the pilot doing the takeoff with flashing lights?"

"Yup, I'd love to sit in the cockpit when Mr. Captain is nosing the plane upward."

"What if it's a woman? Teachers say to use those gender-neutral terms." I try not to smirk.

All he does is shrug and zonk out.

Five minutes of quiet—that's all I'm praying for. Even world peace gets at least that.

I get up to stretch when the person behind me also stands to reach a bag from the overhead bin. The bag nudges me coming down, so I shift my position and grab the luggage tag. It's got a small blob on it that could be a turtle. But nahh, it can't be. Lately I'm seeing them everywhere I go, like when I learn a new word.

As I sit down, Kipp's seat is leaning back too far, so I turn around. "Sorry."

Two men give me blank looks instead of smiles. The brochures say that English and Chinese are the official languages in Hong Kong if that's their destination. The people there speak Cantonese Chinese and may understand other dialects.

I try a little Mandarin Chinese, the most widely spoken dialect. No reaction from them.

So much for the phrases I learned in heritage class. My pronunciation still stinks.

Kipp wakes up and complains his feet feel two sizes bigger, so Mom insists we start the Ankle Alphabet to prevent swollen feet. He shows off by twirling both ankles at once and afterward, walks down the aisle wearing only his socks.

I whisper, "Mom, if I take my shoes off, my socks will get dirty. I'm also stuck on *W*. Move the second stroke all the way up? Or, go halfway up before heading back down?"

She gives me the parent-grin whenever I ask silly questions. "Don't sweat the small stuff. Now, for someone like Kipp, slowing down is a good idea."

I can tell she's starting the meat of her message, so I might as well help. "So that's why you had him pick up popcorn with chopsticks?"

"That obvious, huh? For you, sometimes it is what it is. If only one sock comes out of the dryer, I don't place an ad to look for its mate."

"I like thinking about everything and taking my time."

"It's a wonderful quality, but don't ignore your instincts either." She reaches over and squeezes my arm. "Sometimes you have to get off the boat and stop being so overanalytical."

"Well—I'll think about it." I go back to my reading and rub my leg.

Mom rolls her eyes and casually pulls out a printed sheet wrapped in a ziplock bag. "Anyhow, for a better workout, try the Ankle Alphabet in cursive."

"That's crazy—the teachers swore we'd never use those funny loops and curly-cues." But, how could I ever tell Dad he lost his company since I couldn't get around with swollen feet? "OK, let me look. Oooh, did the plane dip a little? I hope I won't need any anti-nausea stuff."

I clutch my tummy while Mom gets me some ginger ale and crackers. She tells me to lean my head back, so I close my eyes.

She'd freak out if I told her my secret plans. I really, really hope Mr. Han reaches someone at the Black Turtle Group. So I can talk to him. Or her. The knots in my stomach are like the ones I had the first time I was up to bat.

No way that Dad's going to lose everything if I can help it. I love Dad. I love Mom. I (gulp) love Kipp. No one's going to kick my family off our own front porch. Or the back patio.

Digging in my backpack, I finger my small family memories box tucked away safely at the bottom. Touching it always makes me feel better. I pull out

Mr. Han's scribbled note that's already copied in my journal.

Seek a place of long-ago wonder
vessels by the sea
fast crawls, British name
gentle breezes, sovereignty

LEAVE it to him to write some fuzzy phrases, just like he did in class, instead of specific places or phone numbers. Maybe he already forgot about me, but I haven't forgotten about him.

He said to keep my head above water. If I committed to helping Dad, luck would follow me.

Much later, we're landing near water—lit up by twinkly, glittering night lights.

My butt hurts.

7

H IS FOR HUMIDITY

"Touchdown," I whisper and nudge Mom who picks up her tote bag and things.

"Who made the goal? What's the score?" Kipp wakes up and flicks his head up.

"No, Mr. Know-it-all sports guy, we've landed."

"Sweet." A little later, he leads the way through the Hong Kong International Airport.

Talk about a mega-modern airport. I thought they only existed in the States. And I'm not used to seeing so many different people, of all ethnicities. The Chinese people here look kinda like me. The three of us push through the terminal and hear French, Italian, and many other languages.

Kipp, who's taking Spanish, says he can kinda understand *Hola, acabo de llegar al aeropuerto.* He thinks that person is saying "Hey, I'm at the airport now."

I hear *Ni hao, wo jiu zai jichang* that's probably the Chinese version.

The men who sat behind Kipp and me walk past us, using their cells and acting like they want to lose us. It must have been torture for them.

Mom puts away our passports after the Customs line and looks at me. I know what's coming. She likes having me practice finding my way around stations and airports if I'm ever lost. She asks in an innocent voice, "Anyone see the baggage claim area?"

"I know—I know." I fling my backpack over my shoulders, look around, and finally point to a sign. "Yeah, it's up ahead—and look, that's the Chinese character for *exit*." I still remember learning from her that the exit sign is my friend.

We're at the Arrival Hall with our luggage where I dart up ahead for the next sign. Hordes of people hold up signs of traveler names. A tall man holds up a sign with the name Elizabeth.

No big deal. With Hong Kong's British ties and all, Lizzie's got to be a popular name. Plus, English is one of the official languages. Many people might have that name in this area of more than seven million people.

When the guy turns, the full name on his sign is visible—Elizabeth P.

That's what Mr. Han calls me. Very big deal.

Someone bumps into my backpack. I fling it off and hold it while standing on my tippy-toes and search the crowds for the man. Too many people are taking pictures with family and friends. Everyone's shuffling around, and I can't see. He's gone.

I was secretly hoping a guy wearing shades would hand me a message telling me where to go and who to see. Instead, a guy has my name on a sign and vanishes.

I don't know whether I should even be scared or not.

"Everything on track, Ellie?" asks Mom who comes up right behind me.

I twitch my head. "Sheesh, you scared me. Uh, yeah, I didn't sleep well on the plane. All these crowds and the bright lights are too much." I head toward an exit sign for shops and a bank and look back to make sure Kipp is following us.

"By the way, have you figured out what places you want to visit?" asks Mom.

"Yup, and I've scoped out all the important travel

things." Under my breath, I mumble, "Except for buses and trains and subways."

Ta-dah—what are little brothers for. Kipp never gets lost because he's got a built-in GPS. Mom says that he likes watching everything wherever he goes and learned directions that way. I can look around all I want, and things can go completely insane with no mental map.

Facing Kipp as he walks up, I say, "Hey, back in LA, the parents said I'm the boss on this trip. I get to choose what to do and where to go."

He whines, a little boy with mismatched buttons on his jammies. "For real? I'm out of here. Mo-om, did you say that to her?"

She nods her head. "Yes, your dad and I did."

Kipp says to me, "And if you're the Chief Tourist el Presidente, what's my title?" Sometimes he says these neat words, but when Mom asks him what Spanish he's learning, he says burritos and nachos. Or, stuff.

Quick, Ellie, give him something he wants. Like now. "What about vice president of, let's say, transportation? You'd be great at being in charge of how we get around."

"You call that a high position?"

"Why wouldn't it be? If you're, what do they call

it, the chairperson of the board of directors, you'd have a higher position than me."

"OK, but you're not the boss of me," pouts Kipp, "and can I pick a place to visit?"

"Deal, but remember Dad said *never* Hong Kong Disneyland." I will not snicker.

"Uh-aw, can I go home?"

Mom breaks her own rule by kinda rolling her eyes and nodding her head like those lazy-eyed sports bobbleheads. She heads to the ATM to withdraw HK$775 after charging 100 US dollars from her account.

Kipp asks, "Is that our allowance for the week?"

"You wish. I'll get more cash later, but why would you need an allowance here?" asks Mom.

"Come on, we'll do chores when we return. What if we're separated from you? We'd at least have money to get home without asking a stranger," I say.

"That won't happen under my watch." Mom laughs and gives each of us 200 HK dollars and says we need to keep track of the accounting.

Great. I've got a mission and people to see. She can't be hovering over me.

Kipp fingers the light green and pink and blue bills. "Hey, this is so like Monopoly play money. And, El, could I keep your share? I wanna do the math on what we're both spending. You said I'm supposed to help you."

Mom and I both gawk at him. A new Kipp.

I might as well keep him busy, so I hand over most of my money but keep a little on me. "OK, I guess so, but don't spend my share."

Kipp's eyes light up before he marches straight to the airport stores and mumbles about buying a gift. "Hey, I'm rich. I could buy T-shirts and toys for Frankie and lots of junk food."

"One T-shirt. One toy for Frankie. No junk food. That $200 is only about $26 US money—you do the math. Please stay away from stores that sell purses and clothing for people with fat wallets." Instead, Mom steers us toward the 7-Eleven store.

"You've got to be kidding, right? At home, I'm not even allowed to spell 7-Eleven." Cat and I sneaked in a few times to the one near my house, and we don't think it's run-down at all. We bought granola bars with chocolate chips and pretended to be regulars.

"The rules here are a little different since we're traveling." Mom blinks a little more than usual. "I'll pick up a local SIM card here. Your dad said the international charges can be deadly, so thankfully we only brought my cell."

As Kipp and I roam the aisles, he says, "Is she

gonna access MLB baseball scores on a special app? I wanna keep up while we're here."

"APPsolutely not. We will not talk about or do sports in Hong Kong. Ever."

"But you said *app*," says Kipp while I ignore him. "Fine, you take the subway, and I'll take the freeway. LA Dodgers—best of the west."

"Yankees—beast of the east." Oops, no sports.

With a shrug, the Vice President of Transportation says, "Come on guys, this way to the Airport Express." Kipp figures out how to use the Octopus metro cards, used to pay for our rides, that'll last a week.

He points to a map of the high-speed rail running through Kowloon and under Victoria Harbour. It'll get us to the main island on the other side where we're staying. The main island has the same name as the entire area of Hong Kong.

Twenty-four minutes later, we're in the Central district in Hong Kong Island. We walk out of the downtown terminal onto the street.

I just about dissolve into the air.

A pan of warm, sticky bathwater must have poured on me. "O.M.G. This has got to be capital H humidity." Even my zits cry for help and wanna return to hot, dry Los Angeles.

Little bro doesn't mind the steamy sogginess as we stand near the red and white or green and white cabs at the taxi stand. Before Mom can stop him, he raises his hand to the first cab in line.

The driver who pulls up stares as if he's wondering who's the head of our family. Kipp's about half a head shorter than me. I'm shorter than Mom. I feel like telling him, though, I wear a girl's size 14, which sounds bigger than my mom's size 8, but that might confuse him.

I stammer some Mandarin Chinese except I get tripped up by the four tones. And I'm not talking about a cell ringtone. It's like this, a word can be pronounced four different ways. That's four different meanings.

The cab driver only gives me a look like I'm speaking a foreign language with him.

Kipp tries speaking some Cantonese phrases from our tour booklet, but the driver frowns and shakes his head. He waves over the next group of travelers.

Seriously? The airport guy holding up the sign with my name disappears. This sweaty island is a steam bath. And now the cabbie ignores us. I hand him a piece of paper. "Sir, does this help?"

He reads our printed map with directions in

both English and Chinese. Chinese writing for all dialects is the same. When he dips his head, it's a go!

Mom and Kipp rush to the back seat while the cabbie places our suitcases in the trunk. When I get in last, he stares at me—big time—and picks up his cell to check out something. He watches me again as if I'm on his radar for maybe a famous teen star.

Shake it off, Ellie, I probably remind him of some other nerdy kid with braces. Someone who might have appeared in a commercial eating double-chocolate cookies.

The driver wordlessly drives us away from the downtown area. His cab snakes up and up through alley-like streets, making a few zigzag turns that have the three of us running into each other like bumper cars. Kipp and I laugh every time it happens, while Mom's so tired she sways with us without complaining.

Skinny high-rise buildings, mostly white or tan or gray, line the insanely steep streets like a thin glove with twenty stick-like fingers. You'd have to pay me to walk up or down those straight-up sidewalks.

At a big guesthouse on a hill, Mom pays the driver and steps away with Kipp and our suitcases. I stay behind a second to pick up trash scattered on the seats.

I practice the Cantonese phrase to thank the driver. "Mgoi saai."

He turns around and hesitates. Pointing at me, he says something in the weirdest tones as if he memorized it. "Syun by the sea."

8

SOUND OF RAIN

EXACTLY WHAT DOES HE MEAN? Grabbing my back-pack, I jump out, kinda panicked.

In a second, the cab zooms down the steep road to a sudden dead end. It screeches to a stop by a street lamp that I swear is on its last breath. After doing a U-turn, it crawls back up the road, barely making a sound, like a creepy shadow in a movie I once saw.

I step back as it slows down to pass me. When the driver rolls down his window, I can almost catch his breath on my cheek.

"Black turtle," he says, forcing a smile and nodding before the cab streaks uphill.

I run a few feet after him, but the road is too steep. "Sir, what do you mean?" I yell as the cab heads left at the corner and disappears into the inky-black night.

I'm spooked.

That's when I remember Mom and Kipp are my backups, even though they have no idea what I'm up to. "Hey, wait up for me," I say, catching up to them as they step into the guesthouse entrance. I've never been so glad to see them.

At our rooms, we kick off our shoes like we're entering the mudroom at home. I don't even unlace my sneakers. I wear a AAA size, so hard to find that when I outgrow my shoes, Mom moans and groans about looking all over to buy me a new pair.

"First dibs on the futon," Kipp says in the front room. "Anyone who tells Dad I'm watching TV is the world's biggest snitch. Hey, El, check out these lights —do they call it washroom?"

"Outta my way." The dollhouse bathroom makes me glad I'm not tall like Dad. Sitting on the closed toilet seat gives me a chance to think about what the cab driver said. Like what does *syun* mean. Mr. Han's note said *vessels by the sea*, not *syun by the sea*.

My English teacher, Ms. Ohara, always says gestures and words in different cultures might be completely different than what we're used to. The driver could have been giving me a message. Like *don't go by the sea.* Or, he was crabby. And crabby sounds much better than thinking about the dark street. Unless he's related to the guy at the airport who held up the sign with my name.

When I come out, Kipp says with a big smile, "Did everything come out OK?"

I ignore him and peek in the bedroom where Mom's unpacking. "Be right back. I'm going to ask about tourist places."

The same nice woman at the office who checked us in gives me directions to the media room. Before leaving, I ask, "Oh, Miss, I'm Elizabeth Pettit. Could you help me with this word? Does *s-y-u-n* mean anything in Cantonese? I don't know if I'm spelling it right. That's what it sounds like to me."

She tells me that Cantonese, like Mandarin Chinese, also has different tones of the same word with different meanings. But she says one meaning is boat.

A boat has to have water nearby. It's possible the cabbie meant *vessels by the sea.*

I trudge around mazes and corridors to finally arrive at the media room. Searching for general info about the BT Group on the Internet isn't easier on this side of the world. All I can find is that it's a "privately held company" founded by two brothers. The article mostly has Chinese writing with their first names in English—Gerard, the CEO, and his brother Walter.

Attention, you two brothers, I'm here.

It's about time to email my bestie.

"Hey, how was your doctor appointment? I made it to HK with Mom (and Kipp), but something weird happened today. Can't tell you everything now. Remember your history paper on Chinese art? Does a black turtle have a special meaning? I bet softball's going great. Hit hard and run fast, E."

Cat's always been able to figure out something I miss. When I got into softball last year, I was worried after dropping a few balls in the outfield. But she discovered I run faster than most batters. That's if I don't strike out. And when I do get a hit, I make a bet with myself that I'll outrun the throw.

Dad introduced me to betting, something Mom doesn't know. I hated learning to add and subtract in school, so he taught me how to play blackjack. He played the dealer while I had to either hit or stand to make my 21.

"Let's get out those cheese twists for betting," he said one weekend, all casual-like.

"Dad, I'll make you a bet," I'd say to him. On Friday I was a math idiot. By Monday I was adding and subtracting those baby numbers like crazy. I told my speechless grade-school teacher—think black-jack . . . think Vegas . . . think educational field trip.

Baby arithmetic was then. Dad might lose his company now.

When I pass the reception office heading back, the same woman calls out, "Hello, a message came in. I believe it's for you."

The envelope only has my name and last initial with a note inside.

"Elizabeth P., I believe you've arrived. I hope to see you briefly tomorrow afternoon at the museum near the boat. Sincerely, Mr. Han."

It's hard to read his scribbles. And there's that word again—*boat*.

Triple-yay that he knows I'm here. Finally. I exhale, knowing he'll help me with everything.

I thank the receptionist. "By the way, have you ever heard of a company called the Black Turtle Group?"

She doesn't answer. But as I'm leaving, she stammers in a whisper before disappearing to the back of the office. "A corporation that everyone's heard of but knows nothing about."

Back in our rooms, I walk in overhearing Mom on the phone.

"Are you sure the paperwork is accurate? . . . worse comes to worse, move to a cheaper place . . . change schools. Say nothing for now . . . I'll tell her they stopped by . . . she's on top of things here and deputized Kipp. All's well. Good night, good morning there . . . me too."

Moving and changing schools. Cannot. Be. True. I storm into the bedroom. "What paperwork are you talking about?"

Mom replies, "Oh, something about health insurance, but it's nothing to worry about. Did you pack that adapter, the special three-pronged one they use here? My phone needs charging."

She loves changing subjects to protect us, but I'm on to her. And I badly want to scream at someone, so I ask Kipp for the adapter. That's when he dumps all his clothes on the floor.

Theory—he's into sports for the clothes. Proof—lots and lots and lots.

"Holy shirts! Why did you pack thousands of tees?" I sniff-sniff the air. "And what's that mudroom perfume? Exactly how did it follow us across the Pacific?"

"It was an accident 'cause Frankie got into my suitcase. Mom said we might not do laundry here, so I came prepared."

"Sheesh. And what's up with those water bottles you lined up by the door?" I ask.

"Dad said to keep water handy." Kipp acts like he follows directions all the time.

"True, he did say that." I return to the bedroom with the adapter, kinda calmed down. "You must be excited about your conference."

Mom only nods, so I know she's worried about Dad. "Jump up and down and laugh when you're happy. Don't nod." Something hits me, and I scream. "Yippee—I said a palindrome."

Kipp runs in and tilts his head like Frankie does when I taught her a few Chinese words.

"They're words that spell the same forward or backward. *Don't nod* is the same both frontward and backward, you know, like the word *noon*."

"That's it? Like the time you screamed *taco cat* from that board game? I thought something big happened, a home run by the Dodgers or something." He mutters "word nerd" and returns to the living room, even slamming the door a little.

Mom says, "By the way, your dad said Cat and a guy named Russ dropped by."

"What?" First day I'm gone, and he shows up at my door. "I mean, Cat probably left something at the house. But hmmm, why Russ?" My tummy twitches and goes all bubbly. It must be showing on my face as Mom gets one of those curious gleams in her eye.

Focus, Ellie. I throw myself on one of the beds and close my eyes. And try to figure out how I can get to the museum with Kipp to meet Mr. Han tomorrow. Without Mom knowing.

When a sudden torrent lashes the concrete walls outside the guesthouse, I rush to the window. I don't like it. In Southern California, we don't have this type of pouring *zaa-zaa* rain. That's the Japanese onomatopoeia I learned in Ms. Ohara's English class. Then there's *potsu potsu* that's like the pitter-patter of a light drizzly rain. I told Kipp, and he ran around the house yelling them over and over again. Such a baby.

I'm a baby, too, if I let *zaa-zaa* rain throw my plans down the toilet.

Lightning-fast pellets plunge down and disappear under a charcoal sky in a place that's totally strange to me. I read once that sometimes people go to dark places to find answers.

Don't tell me I have to go out there to save Dad's company.

I yank the window drapes shut.

DAY TWO

9

FIVE SECONDS

"Mom, could I use your cell since you'll have phones at your workshops?" I want to make sure she won't get suspicious. Jet lag hit me big time, so it's not like I'm alert yet this morning.

I continue, "Kipp and I could leave messages with the guesthouse office when we go outside. It's supposed to rain a little, but we still can't stay in reading the entire time."

"Hmm, that's right. Today's the busiest day with workshops here and there, mostly in the afternoon. I was planning to run back and forth and see you in between." She's in her planning mode, going over the pros and cons, like she always does. "With your suggestion, I guess I won't have to worry about that. Good, good. That's all settled."

I glide away and mumble ever so softly, "Kipp and I will explore downtown Central by ourselves. I'm gonna take more risks."

Mom's hearing is so good, she clutches her back as if I'd said, "I'm gonna break four discs." She digs her socked foot into the carpet like a pitcher on the mound. "Wait a minute, Ellie, I never said you could."

"You agreed." I take my stand.

"Am I sensing an attitude?"

"You and Dad said I could be in charge the night we bought the tickets."

She says, "All right, but for today only, you're restricted to walking in the downtown area where lots of people are around. Ready? Let's go down and eat."

Mom, Kipp, and I grab a table in the dining room. The speaker system blares, "Attention all guests, breakfast will close in thirty minutes."

"That's a cool announcement," Kipp says. "You can change that to 'Attention all lacrosse players, out on the field in five.' Or, almost anything. Hey, are those pastries?"

"Good thing we made it in time. By the way, no sweets. And don't forget to get right back on that guesthouse ride after you're done exploring downtown." Mom gives our room number and orders a coffee to go. She gets up to leave for the building next door. "Bye, see you later—make good choices."

I yank Mom's sleeve. "Yoo-hoo, your cell, please. Remember?"

"Righhht." She fishes it out of her tote.

We tug back and forth on it. I'm thinking it's any old thing, and she's acting as if it's her favorite takeout menu engraved in gold. Finally, when I'm ready to get a crowbar, she drops it in my palm and heads out.

Kipp scans the menu. "We missed the English breakfast. Want the Chinese breakfast or the Chinese breakfast?"

"Isn't that the same thing?" I ask.

"But Mom said to make good choices."

"That's insane. At least this isn't one of those continental breakfast things with juice and a roll. I'm starved." I smile at a woman with neatly combed jet-black hair who waits for our order.

"My . sister . and . I . would . like . the . Chinese . breakfast . please," Kipp says, speaking loud and clear. After she leaves, he says, "I'm sure the waitress understood me."

"You don't have to talk like that. They speak English here—it's an official language," I say, all disgusted. "And Mom would say she's a server. It's gender-neutral."

"My bad. But the cabbie last night only knew Chinese. And remember, you're not the boss of me."

"OK, maybe not everyone speaks English. And when did I ever say I was your boss? As if." I toss my head.

Soon I breathe in the steam from a thick rice porridge. Swish it around. Try it. Burn my lips a little. Yummy shredded beef slices melt in my mouth. So do the tiny, pickled cucumber bits and sliced scallions sprinkled on top. I don't even care if a few get tangled in my braces.

Picking up my mini roasted meat bun is another story. I miss the cheap, wooden chopsticks we get with takeout food. The long, elegant chopsticks come with attitude—cool as ivory and slippery as ice. One bun wiggles free, flips over, and plops on the carpet.

I groan. "Sheesh—a perfect 10 in the disaster category."

"Five-second rule." In a flash, Kipp picks up the meat bun off the carpet with his hand. And wipes it on his I'M NOT CRAZY, JUST DIFFERENT T-shirt. He takes a bite and smacks his lips.

"Eww." I kick his shoe, but that makes him swallow the whole thing. Gone.

The dining room TV blares, "Market shares . . . Stay tuned for the latest BBC updates . . . In other business news, details on the Black Turtle Group's proposed takeover of a California firm were leaked today. Sources say industry secrets were stolen."

I freeze. California firm. What industry secrets?

A person at the next table gets up and changes the channel to a cricket game.

I push away my food, shove back my chair, and race out of the dining room.

"About that meat bun I ate off the floor—it just happened," Kipp blabs, trotting to keep up with me while stuffing more food in his mouth. "Don't rat me out to Mom."

"What are you talking about?" I shout, taking the stairs two at a time like nobody's business. Fumble, fumble—my key decides it's on vacation before the door unlocks. I flick on the TV and hear an English TV channel reporting, "BT Group's management denies—"

"Keep that channel on," I yell and rush to the bedroom to look for my little black journal. Grabbing it from the dresser, I return to the front room.

"See, that batsman wears lots of gear, almost like ice hockey players," says Kipp.

"What part of *keep that channel on* don't you understand? Where's the news?" I wrestle with the TV remote to change the channel and fail. "I was gone under five seconds."

"How come you don't like watching cricket?"

"Ohhh, you!" I leave and collapse on my bed, squeezing my face with both hands. And think back to the BBC news report on the plane. It reported the Black Turtle Group has a design subsidiary. Dad explained once that's a related firm controlled by the parent company.

Today's report is something new and different. There's no way I can sit around.

When I return to the living room, I growl, "Isn't it a horribly humid day to play cricket?"

"They're reruns—the season is way past." Kipp snickers. "That bowler is pitching fast to the batsman. So, he's got to hit the ball while defending those three wooden stumps—"

"Called a wicket, and yeah, it's one of the most popular sports in the world." I sigh. "My heritage teacher Mr. Han always shared his cricket stories—he grew up here. Look, we've got to catch that guesthouse ride and check out a museum."

Kipp crosses his arms. "Is it a sports museum, and how long ago did cricket begin?"

"Wait, what'd you say? Be back in a minute, so get your stuff ready." I dash up to the media room, after making two wrong turns, and grab some museum brochures and maps.

Checking my email, I read a message from Cat.

"Ellie, don't freak out about the black turtle. It's a sub-sign of the Chinese water element connecting an animal to your birth year. Someone probably thinks of it as a nickname for you. Write when you can. Doc appointment all good for my leg. Get a hit —never quit, C."

I write back.

"Thanks! BTW, I heard Russ stopped by my house. Why, why when I'm away? LOL, E."

Back at my guesthouse rooms, the brochures show many large museums in Kowloon across the harbor. Lots of trekking here and there. Scary directions, traffic, subways.

I need backup. From he-who-has-a-built-in-GPS.

"Can you keep a secret?" I'm quiet as Kipp fixes his eyes on me. "Daddy's company is sorta in trouble, and he'll probably lose everything."

Kipp's face changes to a look he had when Frankie got hurt once. His eyes puddle up, and snot drips from his nose. "Who's the bad guy? I'm gonna give him a karate chop."

"Listen, you can never do that. In LA, I already talked with Mr. Han, the teacher I told you about. He's trying to help me find a top manager from a company called the Black Turtle Group. The news said something about industry secrets being leaked. That's when you switched the TV channel to watch cricket."

"My bad—will we have to move? You're telling me this because of what?" He looks at me with eyes that beg me to protect him.

That gets me every time.

"Keeping this a secret was killing me, so I could use your help." I pat Kipp's shoulder and explain what happened after my heritage class. "Anyhow, Mr. Han sent me a message at the guesthouse asking me to meet him. I'm guessing it's the history museum."

"Bo-rrring. OK, I'm in, but it better have a gift shop." Kipp changes to a clean T-shirt that says LIFE IS BETTER WHEN YOU STICK TOGETHER and gets busy with the tourist maps. "So, me and you, a team."

A little later, we board the guesthouse bus when the driver looks at us curiously. Even if we kinda blend in from the outside. Or, is he staring at my silvery turquoise braces on my teeth?

He asks me, "Are you Chinese?"

"I'm American. But I'm Chinese, too."

"You speak Chinese?"

"No, but I know a few words." Here it comes. He's going to act like it's a sin I don't really know the language and all that.

But all he says, while smiling, is "I hope you have a pleasant trip."

We get off in Central where the humidity is yucky. It's like gobs of glue sticks are smeared all over my body.

Kipp leads the way through downtown. "This way, El. Let's go kick butt."

10

NINE DRAGONS

HONG KONG IS SUPPOSED to have about 300 skyscrapers. Maybe the private BT Group has offices nearby. With a moat around it.

Kipp uses his umbrella to point out landmarks. "See that tall building on the left and the tall building on the right—they could be goalposts on a field. I'll intercept the ball and do a pick-six. So sweet." He can put a sports spin on anything.

I'm going to play along. "Where would the nets on a lacrosse field be?"

"Come on, get real, El. Don't you know the difference between football and lacrosse? Anyhow, you'd need room to play behind the net for lacrosse."

"Behind the net? That's crazy. Listen, we've got to

rush to that museum. If we're late, we'll have to catch the second ride back. I'll leave a message for Mom, so she won't worry," I say. "Ugh, it's starting to rain off and on again."

Kipp says, "How come she and Dad don't know your plan?"

"Do you want to move? Not me. Ever! So, I wanted to take action and asked Mr. Han for some advice. If I told the parents, they would have said I was too young and all that," I say. "It was scary, so I'm glad we're a team now."

At a nearby bus stop, Kipp and I gawk at tons of people boarding a double-decker. We've never seen those in Los Angeles. We also peer in glass-windowed buildings with stores that have mannequins wearing movie-star clothing. Those we've seen plenty.

As we head toward the subway, the Vice President of Transportation pulls out his handy-dandy clipboard welded to his wrist. The title he got at the airport fits him.

I sigh and say, "Don't tell me you packed your clipboard. Did you bring anything useful on this trip?"

A gust of wind whooshes through the downtown

street along with some serious raindrops. Kipp screams and jumps up and down. "My umbrella's half dead and all my stuff is wet."

As if I need this. The great wind-and-rain crisis isn't covered in my *Little Brothers for Dummies* manual. I refold his umbrella and dry off his slightly damp clipboard.

He watches me. "I said be careful. You forgot that corner. Don't forget the back."

Yeah, I let him boss me around because I'm afraid otherwise, he won't behave. Like helping me save Dad's company. Sheesh—little brothers.

Outside the subway entrance, Kipp explains everything like I'm an idiot. "El, this is the MTR. Technically it's the Mass Transit Railway. Look, the subway logo has two north-south semicircles with a vertical line through the center."

Talk about pushing for higher pay. But big sisters have to take the good with the technical. And he knows I tend to get lost, so it's kinda sweet.

We enter the subway. Boy, are we glad all the signs include English.

Kipp has his cheesy grin back on and finds the Red Line that goes to the tip of Kowloon. After swiping our metro Octopus cards, we get on, pretending to be with a tour group that includes lots of kids.

At the harbor stop, we walk through a brightly lit walkway that has codes for the different MTR exits to the streets above. All's good until we see stores near the escalators going up to the street. Uh-oh.

I grab Mr. Shopaholic for a U-turn and point to a big, oversize wall map he starts poring over while I pretend to study it. I'm jealous he can find his way anywhere. Usually he knows where he's going, even in the dark. I'm mostly in the dark about where I'm going, even in the daytime.

We exit and pop up on Nathan Road where the street sign says so in English and Chinese characters. Lots of tourists walk around this part of Kowloon called Tsim Sha Tsui. What can I say, it's so different from the sleeky office buildings in downtown Central. Jammed buses, cabs, and other cars stream up and down cramped streets. Buildings have flashy neon signs using Chinese characters in fonts I've never seen. I only recognize a few characters.

But there's one big difference about Kowloon. I love that it's nice and flat.

"Kipp, c'mon, let's stay close together. This crowd is too much for me." We join a whole wall of people who take up half a block to cross Salisbury Road, one of the busiest streets I've ever seen. Beyond that, Victoria Harbour separates Kowloon from Hong Kong Island where we started from. To the right, a clock tower stands tall overlooking the boats in the harbor.

"Bummer," says Kipp, looking at a map. "The art museum is up ahead, but the history museum is a few miles north. I don't think the MTR goes up there, and the bus might be too slow. How about we take a cab?"

"I'll think of something to tell Mom, but we have to get there first." I kind of poke Kipp in front of me. "Let's hope she'll be happy we're going to any museum." This time he shows our cabbie a map. We're sooo happy when he nods.

I hop into the back seat when Kipp shouts he's running back out to pick up his dropped umbrella. From the rearview mirror, the cabbie flicks his eyes at me.

What's his problem? We lock eyeballs. His face looks like a question mark during our silent staring battle. When he glances at his cell on the dashboard, I look too.

A full-screen picture of a girl with long, dark

brownish hair shows up. She's holding a navy-and-green plaid backpack.

That's me. At the Arrival Hall of the airport.

The bottom of the picture has a tiny line of Chinese words I can't read. Above that is a blinking message in English, "Will delete in 1 hour." Like I'm supposed to be happy about that.

Pointing to his cell, I blurt out in a shaky voice, "Excuse me, why is my picture there?"

He either won't answer, or we don't speak the same language. He doesn't say anything but instead, smiles and nods his head toward the door as if to say, "Get out of the cab, Missy."

I'm half out of the cab with the door open so I can think. It's the perfect time to honor my kindergarten torture days by retying my shoelaces. First my right sneaker. Tie my laces. Now tighten laces on the left sneaker. The cab driver guns his motor—vroom, Vroommmm, VROOOMMMM.

He wants me to get out. Now.

After I shut the door, the cab disappears as Kipp walks up with his mouth open. "Why did you let him go?"

I feel like exploding but pinch myself to not frighten him. "Uh, I think he was in a rush to go somewhere. I'll ask that family over there to help us." I'm grateful when they tell us which bus to catch to the history museum, especially when one comes right away. It's only supposed to take a few minutes. Not nearly enough time for me to stop freaking out about the cabbie.

During our short ride, I try to calm down by telling Kipp the story I read about Kowloon's name. "An emperor saw eight mountain peaks to protect him from his enemies. At first, he called the place eight dragons. But after a guard reminded him the emperor was also a dragon, guess what? He named it nine dragons, which is what Kowloon means."

"That's cool."

At our stop, the museum entrance isn't obvious, so Kipp takes the outdoor escalator to search for it. I walk up to the the street sign, Chatham Road South, to make sure we're at the right place.

When I retrace my steps, I freeze. The cabbie's back—parked on the street where the sputter of the car motor gives it away. He must have followed our bus. His cell flashes wildly in his hands when he turns and sees me. He'll probably report me to the Weird Taxi Passengers Department. Well, almost a passenger.

They'll plaster my face all over on a poster, and my cover will be blown. Except wait. My face already shows up on his cell and maybe the cells of other drivers. Maybe that's how the airport driver from last night might have recognized me. He was looking at me so weird, like he had seen me before.

My sweaty forehead feels as if hot water from the shower dumped on me.

I jump on the escalator. At the top, Kipp is leaping over puddles in front of the museum. I'm scared, but I don't want to scare him. I mean, he's not even ten yet.

Trying not to shiver, I describe my picture on the cabbie's cell. "Before you and I became partners, a guy at the airport held up a sign with my name *Elizabeth P*. That's what Mr. Han calls me."

"That guy probably took a picture of you."

"No kidding. And if Mr. Han is trying to reach me, he sure has a funny way of doing it. Now we've got to hurry, so let's stick together." I fly into the museum from the rain forest, a sticky cinnamon bun ready to shower off. "Oooh, I love air conditioning."

"Would you marry it?" Kipp asks, right behind me.

I do the perfect little-brother shrug, imitating the master who does it best in the whole world. After standing in line, I get ready to ask Kipp for some of my cash, but—surprise—the admission fee is super cheap.

When we head toward the exhibits, the cell rings. Mom's having a cow. "What do you mean you missed that ride? Where are you?"

"The guesthouse bus must have come early, so we kinda didn't see it. Kipp and I decided we should be safe and sort of followed a tour group on the subway across the harbor." She doesn't have to know that we almost took a cab ride. "Mr. Han said to visit this history museum on the first day since time passes fast during trips."

"Honestly, Ellie, do you ever listen to me? And don't use that tone of voice with me."

"But Mo-om, I'm already twelve. I left you a message like you asked me to. And it's not like we secretly took a bus to another state, like those kids in that book you read to us." I roll my eyes a little, knowing how dangerous it is to do that. All kids know that moms have cameras in the back of their heads.

"I saw that, Ellie." Her four words jump out loud and clear.

See what I mean? "I'm sorry, but you don't have to yell."

Her voice sounds croaky as she says quietly, "I

don't have time to argue. The local parents at the workshop say it's safe for you and Kipp to return by yourselves. It would take longer for me to go get you. Please confirm with the security guards the nearest exit and get back."

"But, but Mom!"

"NOW."

11

SAMPAN MODELS

"WE'LL GET BACK across the harbor and pick up the last guesthouse ride." I nod and give a wobbly thumbs-up to Kipp.

"When you return, Elizabeth, we're going to have to talk." Click.

It's never good when moms sit you down for the talk. But it's worth breaking a few rules as long as mine doesn't send me packing on the next plane to Los Angeles.

"Kipp, we're so dead. Mom wants us to get back now, no matter what. But Mr. Han's note said he'd meet me in the afternoon." Sigh, that could be now or in the next several hours. "Look, let's start with those exhibits featuring archaeology and stuff."

"You mean stuffology." He and I look at the

museum's layout while I try to clamp down my smile. If my parents were here, they'd be secretly proud that he's witty. That means kids have to walk a real tightrope most of the time.

Correction, all the time.

The exhibits are the most awesome things ever. I know Cat would love them, too, as she loves all things history. Viewing them and wondering where Mr. Han will show up drives me bananas. I don't know what to concentrate on. But I do try to memorize things to write down in my journal later for Dad. And also try like crazy to not think about the cabbie's weird stares.

Kipp reads off an exhibit card about the Han dynasty rule of over 400 years—all with different generations of one family. "Kinda like sports dynasties. Now we're talking."

"That's silly. Why would sports dynasties have anything to do with that?" Hmmm. "But wait, dynasty is kinda like sovereignty, one of the words on Mr. Han's scrap of paper. He wrote *gentle breezes, sovereignty*. Hold that thought. We've got to hurry."

On a sloping walkway, I almost miss the glass plaque taking up half the wall. Most people don't even stop to glance at it. Except for a nerdy reader like me who loves reading, but not off a boring list.

"Kipp, quick, come here. Look at the list of museum donors. I can't believe I'm seeing the Black Turtle Group's name up there. At least now, I'm sure Mr. Han meant this museum."

"Yeah, a real mega-bucks company." He squints at the tiny lettering on the plaque.

We move on to the next level of exhibits. While reading the info card, he says, "Lookit, this sampan is the size of a real one."

Sampan. Boat. Syun, the Cantonese word for boat. In front of us is a flat-bottomed replica. The real ones, this size, are used for fishing or for getting around the Hong Kong islands.

A rickety roof strapped down with tarp covers about half the boat. Outside on the deck, a mannequin holds a long pole, as if the man is propelling the boat. A low straw hat hides his face.

I lean over and pick up a crumpled piece of paper on the deck and crush it in my pocket. Might as well keep the museum clean.

"Mr. Han's message said to meet him at the museum by the boat. He's so absent-minded, it'd be like him to come up with such an obvious message," I say.

"Yeah, as obvious as runners beating the throw to

first base. Here, let me check it out." Kipp tries to get on the sampan.

I whip my head around to see if anyone's watching us. "Are you crazy? OK, here, I'll lean down while you kneel behind and grab hold of my legs." I peer in the living area that has all of the family belongings. And come face-to-face with a life-size mannequin sitting on the floor, folding blankets.

Hello, lovely woman on a sampan. You're taking care of your family. And I want to take care of mine.

"Kipp, let's go. I don't see anything and don't even know what I'm looking for. Plus, no one's around on this level of exhibits."

We whirl through the others before heading back to the main level. Kipp hustles to the one museum section my parents dread—gift shop. I overhear him whispering to the cashier about something "beads," but the cashier shakes her head.

As if any almost-fifth-grader needs to buy jewelry. But what do I know? It's another subject not covered in my *Little Brothers for Dummies* manual.

Past the gift shop entrance, a nearby museum attendant by a podium smiles and waves me over. Me?

Wait, am I stupid or what? He'll tell me where to meet Mr. Han. What I'm here for. Duhh.

When I speed up to him, he says, "Hello, we welcome you to learn about our history and culture. This may be yours." He hands me my travel journal.

"My journal, how did it drop out? Thank you so much."

"Where are you traveling from? I detect an American accent."

I didn't know I had an accent. I thought everyone else did. "I'm American, but my grandparents are from China."

"I hope you are enjoying the exhibits," he says, smiling.

"Absolutely! I especially like the life-size models of the woman and man on the sampan."

He nudges his glasses up. "That's one of my favorites, too. But that particular exhibit has only one mannequin model—the woman inside the sampan."

"No, I'm positive a model of a man, too, is standing on the deck. He had on a straw hat and was holding a pole as if to steer the boat."

"Only one model, a woman." He looks puzzled as his arm moves down behind the podium.

I'm literally sweating now. If he calls security, Mom will ground me for life—and I won't get the new cell she promised.

Instead, the attendant shows me a brochure of the sampan exhibit. It's got only one model.

"Uh, OK." But it's not OK. I shove my hand in my pocket. "Wait, here's a piece of paper I picked up next to the guy with the straw hat. Can you tell if it's trash or not? I can't read the Chinese characters."

He looks down at the note. "Thank you, young lady, for keeping our museum clean. Oh, these words are nonsense—*fast crawls.*"

That's a line from Mr. Han's note. I mumble and grab back the piece of paper. "I'll keep it as a souvenir. Thank you. Mgoi saai."

After splitting, I tell Kipp to stay in the gift shop no matter what—as if he'd ever leave—and scramble around different levels and walkways back to the sampan exhibit. My eyes are glued to the deck when the lights flicker and dim. I snap my head back.

A room ventilation system gives a slight whirring sound. The lights go out completely. Spooky. I duck down and hunch my shoulders. I can hear my nostrils flaring. It's that quiet.

All I want is to make a quick get-away. NOW.

After taking a deep breath, I get up when I sense my entire arm was lightly scrubbed. Rough as burlap and cool as straw hidden from a scorching sun all day. A person brushed by me for real.

The lights flicker and come back on as I blink and touch my face to prove I'm me. I'm sooo happy other people are walking around.

"Hello?" I call out as I peer into the sampan and see the model of the woman. The deck is empty, but in front of me, a long stalk of straw is lying on the floor where I was crouching.

That's when I move away without actually running. I don't want to call attention to myself, but I don't know where I'm heading. Mom's words flash in my brain—the exit sign is my friend.

Until a voice rings out.

"Ah, Elizabeth P., is that you?"

"Mr. Han, I'm sooo happy to see you! You're actually here?" I relax after holding my breath for so long.

He waves at me, wearing his usual baseball cap on messy blackish-grayish hair. "I described you to a museum employee who thought you'd be here."

"How were you able to get me that message at the guesthouse?"

He chuckles. "Happily, life is full of coincidences. I know people who sat near you on your flight. Not knowing your schedule, I gave you a little nudge here and there like at the airport."

"That wasn't exactly a nudge. The guy at the airport put up my name and disappeared. The cab driver the first night spit out some words and sounded scary. Before the bus ride to the museum, I saw another cabbie with my photo on his cell like everyone is searching for me." I let out a whooshy breath. I didn't even realize how confused and kinda scared I was.

"It's they who were frightened without speaking English well, trying to help me find you. I am truly sorry if it was confusing or in any way alarming." Mr. Han leans forward. "The last cab driver only phoned to say you were here. Things aren't always what they seem."

"Funny, that's what my dad tells me all the time. But what about this odd note?" I show him my crumpled paper.

"Oh, that? One of the employees here can get so melodramatic. In case I missed you, I told him to give you a message, and here you are. Please forgive me as I didn't mean to leave you in a lurch. But I had last-minute delays in LA—my health for one thing."

"Are you all right?"

"I have bad numbers. The doctor reported my

cholesterol level spiked to 280. That was when we talked in LA the last time. I'm sorry to bore you as kids don't know about these things."

"That's so not true. My mom is always worried about my dad's cholesterol 'cause she thinks he's getting pudgy. But, you're nowhere close to that." I tilt my head.

"That's what shocked me. In addition to my family medical history, stress can compound things. I must be careful since high cholesterol can sometimes result in heart attacks or strokes." Mr. Han ignores his buzzing cell and smiles at me peacefully, like grandfathers know how to do best. If he is a grandfather. "When the heart is at ease, the body is healthy. Now, let's talk about you."

"I'm in the doghouse with my mom big time. I couldn't tell her I was meeting you, and I've got to leave right away. By the way, did you ever call that manager at BTG?"

Mr. Han stops smiling. Instead, he has the saddest look ever and talks in a low voice. "He and I haven't been in touch for a few months. I'll try reaching him, although we haven't gotten along lately. The person I know best is Gerard."

"What—the CEO? Which office does he work in Central?"

12

TAKE RISKS

"Office? Forget that. Who can get through his security wall?" He wipes his forehead.

"Well, then, how—?"

"He likes to work out. Your best chance to reach him is visiting a fitness center, perhaps one with a pool. He most likely goes when it's not crowded, so I'd find a place you're familiar with."

"But I'm not familiar with any places here." Like is he serious? I fidget with my headband.

"Try your best and take risks. Gerard and I aren't talking, so it's the best I can do."

"I'll try, and oh, I almost forgot. Please don't call or text since I share my mom's cell on this trip. She'd go ballistic if she knew what I was doing." I look for a pen from my backpack. "Could I email you if something comes up? I can do that at the guesthouse where you left a message for me."

"Certainly, and I'm getting a new cell soon, so here's a temporary email. But I want to warn you it's hectic now as I get resettled and start new volunteer work. I don't routinely check for messages and texts the way others do." He scribbles something down and hands it to me, folded. "Please remember—Gerard is the one you must meet."

Yeah, if I can find him. "Sheesh, I almost forgot to tell you. The news reported BTG is accusing my dad's company of stealing industry secrets. What could that be?"

"Gerard would be the person with answers." Mr. Han's cell buzzes again, and he rubs his forehead. "Ah, Elizabeth P., you've done so much by traveling all the way here. And now I must leave."

"So, he's your contact, but you're not talking." I'm trying hard to figure out what any of this means. "I really want to help my dad."

"Loving your family and wanting to help is the right thing to do. And for that, you'll take risks—we all do. I hope you get a good taste of Hong Kong." He turns to leave.

I don't want him to go. "Mr. Han, are you saying I have to eat more?"

His face breaks out into a big smile. "I forgot you have a way with words. Anyhow, finding your way means getting lost first. I believe in you, and now, believe in yourself." He glides out of sight.

I stare at him, kinda confused, and return to the gift shop.

Kipp gets growly like Frankie when I poke him toward the main lobby. "Geez, the lights went off a little while ago. That cut into my shopping time."

I whisper, "Mom's waiting back at the guest-house, and we have to leave n-o-w to try and catch the last guesthouse bus."

We rush out and backtrack to Central. On the subway, I get out Mr. Han's note.

Since baak nin
alive with swimmers
glittering sights and
nighttime glimmers

WHY, oh, why does he keep doing this? He couldn't say in a simple way, "Hey, do this and that." Instead, his note is puzzling as the phrases he said in heritage class. Before we left Los Angeles, Dad told me not to sweat the small stuff, so I'm going to have to think of another plan fast. Unless this is as good as it gets.

I tell Kipp my teacher hasn't been talking to his main contact, the CEO, for several months. I groan. "Why would Mr. Han suggest talking with him if they don't get along? He seemed upset and sad about it, too." We walk to the pick-up point for the bus.

Kipp pretends to take snot from his nose, rolls it, and shoots his basketball into an imaginary net. "Maybe they fight like we do sometimes."

"Ewww, stop with the snot shot. Grown men fighting in a corporation? Get real. Quick, there's our bus ride." I grab Kipp's arm—not his contaminated hands—and nudge him.

When Kipp and I walk into our guesthouse rooms, Mom cries out and scoops us in her arms. That's before she hustles me into the bedroom. "I was so frightened about what you did. If I hadn't asked other local parents about your safety, I'd have gone berserk."

"We saw lots of kids here and there. What'd I do wrong?" My chin starts quivering. "It's like going from one end of our town to the other."

"I can't have you two wandering off by yourselves in a strange place. I've got enough on my plate." Her voice softens.

"Mom, I'm sorry, but you said I could be in

charge. They speak English here, and Kipp and I were safe the whole time."

"Let's all calm down, and look, I didn't mean to get angry." She tries hard not to yell at me. "The good news is I adjusted my schedule to attend only the early morning workshops. When you two sleepyheads get up, we'll be together for all activities."

OH. NO. I love Mom, but if she latches herself on to me here, I might fail. And Mr. Han said he'd be unreliable and busy. Quick, Ellie, think fast. "That's fine, uh, and didn't you say in LA you have a friend who lives here? Are you getting together with her?"

"When I thought I wasn't coming, I canceled. I believe she's also traveling this week. Why?"

"Um, I wouldn't mind asking a local person about places to visit we might not know about." I straighten my clothes in the dresser, thinking "Yesss," after Mom says she'll try to reach her.

That night as I'm about to enter the bedroom, she's talking to Dad. He must have gotten up at dawn to phone her as it's yesterday in Los Angeles.

"So glad you called. How're you doing? What? . . . Everyone's starting to pack up their office belongings? Don't worry, we'll make things work . . . Wait, are you certain? When the health insurance is canceled, can you figure out the cost of that temporary, expensive one? . . . Don't worry about it, everything's fine, talk later. Love you."

I rush in and signal to talk to him. Mom looks awful as she hands me the cell I take into my bathroom office. "Dad, how's it going?"

"You first. Are you and the Kippster having a good time?" His voice sounds faint and tired.

"Yup, and guess what—we went to an incredible museum today. What's up with the health insurance Mom was talking about?"

"She wants to keep the same plan to stay with Kipp's allergist, but we're a small company with limited coverage options." Dad sighs. "By the way, I realize you're aware my company is being taken over. I have to sign some documents before it's finalized."

That's the worst news ever. Like I'm shaking. "What happens to our family?"

"Don't worry—I'll find work but possibly at quite a distance from our present neighborhood. In today's world, company takeovers and mergers are common occurrences. I only wish it wasn't happening at lightning speed."

"Dad, we love you, and we'll be home in a couple of days. So, please don't sign anything yet. I'll even

take up your advanced blackjack course if you don't
—promise?"

All he says is "Listen, Ellie, absolutely no betting
while you're there. And don't forget to write down
your impressions of the museum as you promised.
Anyhow, let me get going here."

He's gone. How's that for not answering my
question.

As I'm about to return to the bedroom, I stop. I
hear crying with gasps that can't quite escape, the
kind when my grandparents passed away.

Moms aren't supposed to cry. When they do, it's a
sign that things are going downhill fast. They read
you stories and show you how to be kind. They hug
you when you're down.

Mom and Dad and Kipp, I love you. Whatever
happens to us, we're still family.

Back I go into the bathroom and turn on the
faucet full blast while sitting on the toilet seat. I cry
for Mom crying and Dad who's about to lose his
dream company. I bawl my head off about not
having my plans work out. Finally, I rinse my eyes
over and over.

When I enter the bedroom, I avoid Mom and
hope she doesn't look too closely at my face.

She straightens up her sagged shoulders and

reaches for the tissue box with her pinkish eyes. "Allergies—this humidity is rough."

"Me, too, and my eyes feel itchy." I give her a big hug for having allergies the first time ever. "Do you feel a little better?"

"Not bad. Let's just say I'm past tense." She grins at me, and we burst out laughing.

"Grammar nerds forever, that's us." What she doesn't see is I'm crying on the inside. "Mom, how come you told Dad things are fine when you were so upset and sad as you talked?"

"At times people don't want to distress others. I stretched the truth a little so he wouldn't be anxious." She climbs into bed and fiddles with the lamp on the nightstand.

"I'll turn off my lights in a little while," I whisper and get out my black journal.

Dear Dad,

Did I ever love the history museum. Lots of exhibits showed Hong Kong's natural terrain and other stuff starting from about 400 million years ago. Kipp liked it, too, and thinks the stuffologists (he means archaeologists) did a cool job.

Hong Kong's people immigrated long ago from China and passed down their cultures and technology. The pottery and paintings from dynasties centuries ago were awesome. I liked seeing things in person about what I covered in heritage class.

The folk culture exhibits were the best. One was a wedding scene where a bride was inside a portable sedan lined with silky red cloth, like the kind Mom once showed me in a fabric store. I could almost feel the smooth golden tassels twitching from side to side when the sedan was carried by lifelike mannequins.

I know Mom's parents are from China. I'm beginning to feel connected to Chinese people here. I'm used to being a Pettit all my life. Now I know something about being a Wei.

Love, Ellie xoxo

Afterward, I take out the contents in my small memory box from my backpack. The last time I opened it was when we touched down in Hong Kong. That was only yesterday.

Family is the only thing that matters.

I pop my head in next door and tell Kipp, "Pssst, Mom and I are going to sleep early."

Little brothers shouldn't hear about moms crying and dads packing up soon.

DAY THREE

13

SWORDS ON THE RIGHT

Why's Russ talking to my dad?

Cat's email message early the next morning makes me wish I was back home.

"Hey, I picked up my hoodie at your place. Russ was leaving as I stopped by. Maybe he was talking to your dad about whatever. Anything new? Holler if you need me. Softball going well. Train insane, C."

The last time I saw Russ was at the little park by my house. I couldn't even catch a lacrosse ball he practically handed me. Did he notice? Ha!

Ellie, Ellie, focus, focus. Dad is a gazillion times more important.

After looking up fitness places in Hong Kong, I return from the media room. When I walk to the bedroom on tippy-toes, Mom is still sleeping like a baby. She must have watched Kipp and me napping so many times when we were little.

Today I'm watching her, and things aren't going well at all.

A slight noise like pens or keys rattles from the bathroom. The kind that sounds like a little kid has a secret. I've read *Little Brothers for Dummies* from cover to cover, so I'm trained.

I wait outside until the door opens. "Boo! Looking for dental floss?"

Kipp is holding Mom's tote and shrugs. "I lost my gender-neutral toothbrush."

"Seriously? In her personal stuff—why?" I grab the bag from him and hang it on the doorknob.

"I've gotta buy something and thought my money was there. Didn't you say you weren't the boss of me?" With a big-boy sneer, he runs to the futon and flops on his pillow. In a minute, he fake-snores as if I can't take a hint he wants to lose me.

Shaking my head, I slip back into bed and read the piece of paper from Mr. Han again. I don't know what the first line means, and the last two are descriptions. I focus on one line—alive with swimmers. If it's about beaches, we're nowhere near them.

And Mom wouldn't let us go anyhow since we live in Southern California where there are tons of them.

But Mr. Han did say to go with what I'm familiar with.

I sit up. How stupid of me.

I know where to go this morning.

After Mom is at her workshop, I make a call. When she returns, I announce, "Guys, we're off to the Hong Kong YMCA across the harbor."

"I always knew I was one of the guys. But, why there, of all places?" she asks.

Kipp coughs and sounds a little wheezy. "Yeah, can I go back to sleep? We go all the time at home, so who wants to come all the way here to check out another Y?"

Exactly—that was Mr. Han's point. "That slow walk through the museum wasn't exactly a workout," I say.

"Sor-ree, I didn't know you were such an athlete."

I mouth the words "Mr. Han" to him and pretend to do swimming strokes when Mom's back is turned. "The Hong Kong Y is supposed to be fancy. It's got a couple of pools and is also a big hotel with meeting rooms and restaurants."

"Restaurants? Fine, let's go. The weather is supposed to be a sunny 31° Celsius today. I forgot what that converts to," says Mom who pretends she needs help in every subject.

Kipp's on it right away. "This here guidebook says to multiply 31 by 1.8, so it'll be 56 degrees Fahrenheit." He looks proudly at Mom who shivers, hinting we didn't pack any coats. "Who said I finished the calculation? Of course, I'm adding 32 to the total. So, about 88 degrees today."

Mom mutters under her breath, "He *is* learning something in school."

"What's with all the math lately? Trying to impress someone?" I ask.

"Numbers count." Kipp grins and shrugs.

"Hmm, it doesn't add up." Maybe it has to do with our neighbor, his friend Wynnie. I grab my softball cap. "The bottom line is we need serious exercise. We need to take risks to get rewards."

"Speaking of not adding up, Ellie, I thought I curbed your excess screen time on the Internet. Since when did you pick up business talk like *bottom line* and *risks* and *rewards*?" Mom tilts her head and seems puzzled. "Those are adult words."

"You mean like books for adults?"

She touches her upper lip, I'll bet, to clamp down any snickers. "Very funny—I meant that grown-ups use those words. All of a sudden, you're into business terms. A different you."

In times like this, kids know how to switch subjects so fast parents never get suspicious. "Maybe I'm training to be an intern at a fancy company. Um, did you hear from your friend about getting together?"

"Not yet. Oh, and you might not have realized it when I first told you in LA. She's the one who recommended Mr. Han's heritage class for you. Come on, let's get going."

Freaking T-shirts. All this time Mom's friend knew Mr. Han. I've got a billion questions to ask her. If she contacts us, I can beg her to help me with a Plan B.

Outside, as we walk up the steep path to the public bus stop, Kipp starts coughing up a storm, so Mom rushes over to him. "This weather might be kicking up that pre-asthma of yours. I'll schedule a doctor's appointment when we return."

Kipp puts his arm out to ward her off. He once said that's a no-no in lacrosse, but off the field, kids want to stop parents from babying them. "Can't I cough a little if I want to? And what if she tells me I have to use an inhaler?"

"It might be a good thing, but let's hope you're not at that stage. Don't overdo anything on this trip." Mom pulls out a tissue to dab her eyes when his back is turned.

I remember last night when she was all upset about the cost of our health insurance. "Take it easy, Kipp." I echo, huffing and puffing as if I've crawled uphill for half a mile. It keeps me from crying at her words.

At the main street I cross the road to the bus stop sign. "Over here, guys."

"El, you're on the wrong side," yells the Vice President of Transportation. "We're going this way, toward downtown in Central. Remember yesterday at the museum—Hong Kong used to be a British colony?"

"You don't have to broadcast that over the entire island. I know that." Yeah, right. I cross the street again and get a crick in my head from looking the other way for oncoming cars.

"Two adolescents—how lucky can I get?" says Mom. "Listen, I read one custom of left-hand driving started during the days of the knights. They had to keep their swords handy with their right hands when traveling in case of an attack."

Kipp says, "So you're saying they drive on the left side of the road but in the right side of the car." He pretends he's riding a horse, reins and all. "You'd see a rider on a horse charging at you, and you both stick your swords out to attack each other. Take that, you knights in my way."

Is he cute or what? But no one, N.O., should ever quote me. Ever.

A minibus rolls up, not one of those double-decker buses I'm dying to ride. Later, we change to the subway going under Victoria Harbour and end up at the tip of Tsim Sha Tsui again. Mom might be impressed I kinda know where I'm going. But I can't say anything to remind her of Kipp's and my independence yesterday.

After we arrive at the Y and Mom arranges for guest passes, I talk plans with my partner. "Don't forget the line from Mr. Han about swimmers. Also, I already checked this is one of the quietest times in the pool."

Afterward, everything goes wrong.

Three people. One pair of goggles.

"First dibs. You had them for a couple of days."

Kipp, who's not exactly a team player, whines and grabs them.

"Are you seriously counting the time it was in my suitcase?" We kick off a tug-of-goggles-war right there in the lobby. Lowering my voice, I say, "Should I tell Mom you were messing with her tote bag?"

He scowls and wordlessly returns the goggles to me.

In the end, Mom plucks them right out of my hands and announces she'll use them. For what? In the locker room, she says, "Would you mind keeping an eye on Kipp in the leisure pool? Without him knowing, of course."

It's one thing when my neighbor Abbey pays me to watch her boys. "Me? I did not sign up for babysitting services in any Hong Kong pools, especially for family members. He already knows how to swim."

"Come on, Ellie, be a big sister. After my workshop sessions, I could use some exercise in the lap pool."

What's wrong with me? "Sure, Mom. I know you're going through a lot—of course I'll watch Kipp." I walk out with a drawstring sackpack that's got my towel and drop it on a bench before stepping into the water.

Several kids in the leisure pool are playing and

splashing around with a baby-pink starfish and an aquamarine seahorse, all made of plastic. Nearby, a gray-and-white dolphin bobs along.

Kipp swims up to me and hisses, "Psst, look at that girl on the far side. What pool toy is she playing with?"

14

CLOSE ENCOUNTER

I TWIST my head and gape at a little girl five or six years old. She's about the age of one of my neighbor Abbey's sons. Playing with a plastic black turtle.

Ms. Ohara always told my English class that colors can mean different things in different cultures. It's still kinda odd, though.

A few parents are reading at the side of the pool, but every so often they look toward the pool. One man with slicked-back hair in a polo shirt follows the little girl with his eyes. I know that look. It's a permanent all-smiley face that's a little bit nervous. Mom and Dad gave me the identical look when I first swam at our family Y.

"Ai-yah," screeches the little girl as the toy turtle

shoots out of her hands and lands with a little splash between her and me.

From my side, I swim across like crazy to grab the toy and fetch it to her. "Here you go."

The man wearing a polo shirt stands, adjusts his glasses, and smiles at her. He turns and looks my way for a nanosecond. If that's a thank-you, I'll take it. Since all's good, he doesn't look at me again after sitting down.

I'm at the side where the grown-ups are sitting and can see him better. He glimpses down at the work he's brought. He's careful about opening his sketch pad, choosy about his pencil.

A sketcher like Dad. This I've got to see.

I focus on him while edging out of the pool to grab my sackpack. After wrapping my towel around my waist, I walk toward him. My flip-flops show off purplish sequins, so dazzling since the day I begged Mom to buy them for me.

Squishy-squish, squishy-squish, squishy-squish.

It doesn't matter because The Sketcher doesn't notice anything or anyone else.

I know that look—concentrating on something in front of you while blocking out all the family noise and other distractions. It's on Dad's face when he's sitting by himself and doodling. Sometimes I shout at him that Mom's whipped up homemade pizzadillas (yeah, right) or scream that Kipp was drafted by the MLB (yay). But does he look up?

Never.

The Sketcher draws the toys in the pool. They're not the same style but kinda similar to what I've seen at home. Dad's been sketching those awhile, especially since Avabrand launched his mini sea animal designs.

A woman with a laptop sitting near The Sketcher has on a shimmering jacket with tiny embroidered designs. A purse that cost my allowance for the decade. And shoes that shout "I'm Italian" leather, like in a catalog I once saw at Cat's house.

She's speaking Cantonese to the man while covering part of her mouth with her hand. It's what baseball catchers do when they run up to the pitchers for a meeting on the mound. I'm like a nervous fan straining to hear what's going on with the game on the line.

When the woman switches to English, she no longer covers her mouth. Instead, she's crunching numbers on her super fancy laptop. "I'll get back to you tomorrow. The other department has almost completed the acquisition of the Kowloon company."

"What is the delay with the workers? I absolutely do not want any miscalculations this time," says the man.

"Many people have relatives also working for the firm, so the total impact would be that much greater." She glances up from her spreadsheet.

"You are new to the company. Please remember that these are merely job changes—it is nothing personal." He almost hisses the words.

"I'll communicate that to the relevant department. When are you next available to meet?"

"Sofie is one tough boss. Let me consult her schedule for visiting the office this week."

Picking up her laptop with hands showing off pretty nails, the woman zips open a case with three gold letters stamped in the corner—B is the first letter. "Fine. Next, we'll wrap up matters on that small firm Avabrand in Los Angeles, Gerard."

Dad's company.

Freaking T-shirts.

That's Gerard—the CEO of the Black Turtle Group. The BBC news on the plane called him "fiercely competitive." Executives talking to other executives, meeting by the Y pool.

Pretty sneaky.

Enemy number one's real close, sitting a few feet away from me.

He might have been the man at the airport holding up a sign with my name. Or was he the cabbie from the first night in downtown Central?

I lucked out. Mr. Han said things would happen if I committed to taking risks, like in softball. But now what? Gerard aka The Sketcher starts packing up like he's getting ready to leave.

Oh, no you don't. I flick my ankle in frustration. One flip-flop jumps off my skinny foot and hits the man's leg before bouncing off. No! Yes.

I take a deep breath going down the gangplank, making my way toward him. "Sorry—it was an accident. My flops are loose 'cause they don't come in triple-A sizes." I grab and put it on.

He pretends not to notice me and glances at his big-bucks watch. His face doesn't exactly announce, "Welcome to Hong Kong." Instead, he treats his drawings like royalty.

"I like those." I point to his sketch pad.

All he does is give me a quick glance and look away. He's too important to talk to me. I'm so nervous I pull my sackpack off my shoulders.

He pulls his head back and glares. Pointing to

one of Dad's tiny sea animal designs on my sack-pack, he asks with a voice like thunder, "May I ask where you purchased that?"

"This? I got it from my dad. He's the art director and owner of Avabrand." Quick, this is my chance to not flub up. "Um, I'm Elizabeth. I have a Chinese heritage teacher in Los Angeles named Mr. Han. I mean I used to, but the classes are over now. Did he ever call you?"

"Excuse me?" he says, while we gawk at each other.

The woman next to him moves over and smiles at me before picking up her laptop case. I don't know if I should take her seat for my business meeting with the CEO.

Splash!

Everyone jerks their heads up and looks at the pool.

He didn't.

He did.

Kipp did a cannonball.

I'm steamed.

The Sketcher's boiling.

Water streaks the top page of his sketch pad. He carefully swabs it with a towel as if he's drying off the crown jewels of England. Next, he wipes off the lens on his tortoise-like glasses before shoving them back on.

He abruptly gets up after calling out something in Cantonese to the little girl who says, "OK, Baba," and they rush off.

Baba, papa, dada, and daddy—the universal names for dad. That's his daughter for sure.

My big break. I came all the way from California, and now this.

When my little bro takes his time coming out of the pool, I scream, "Kiippp! Why? A cannonball here, of all places. Even the lowest stuffologists wouldn't do that."

He doesn't say a word.

"Craziest thing ever. Didn't anyone tell you about timing?" I throw my hands in the air.

"I missed that day at Cannonball School."

I lower my voice. "That's not funny. I'm sure that was Gerard, the CEO of the Black Turtle Group. Now he's gone, and we've got so little time. Don't you want to help Daddy?"

"I love him as much as you do." Kipp's big eyes puddle up as he slides back in the water without a ripple. He avoids looking at me and glides away.

I stalk out of the pool area, yelling out, "Could you

please get out in a few minutes? I'm leaving." In the locker room, I throw my clothes on and cram my swimsuit, towel, and sackpack in my backpack before zipping out to explore the main floor. I even have my pretend sword ready on the right, but I don't see Gerard.

I must be having another slow light bulb day—blame it on jet lag flying into the eastern hemisphere. Wouldn't Gerard and his daughter be leaving soon? I race back to the lobby and peer out the window by the front entrance.

A glistening black limo is parked out front, while a chauffeur places some sports bags in the trunk. I split outside to get a better view when a window rolls down, and the little girl from the pool waves at me.

I wave back. I've got a friend.

Her hand is yanked in, and the window closes.

I should have thought of a different way to talk to the CEO by the pool. My big chance to help Dad goes down the drain.

And now, Gerard is gone.

When I return to the area outside the locker rooms, two people are waiting for me. One doesn't look very happy. At all.

"Ellie, I found your little brother waiting here by

himself. Didn't I ask you to stick together?" Mom frowns.

"I. don't. need. a. babysitter." Kipp looks at me with eyes begging me not to say anything about the pool fiasco.

She has a right to be angry, but he is my partner. I ask to speak to her alone down the hallway as he watches us with narrowed eyes.

"Mom, he's right. He doesn't need a babysitter. He even helped someone who lost her pool toy. I left early because I got dressed in a hurry and wanted to explore a little."

"What? Without telling him where you were going?"

"It's a long, weird story." And I'm already down in the dumps.

The sweetest mom who used to tuck me into bed now stands like a ten-foot wicked ogre, folding her arms. "Try me—I like long, weird stories."

15

SWIMMERS ON THE LEFT

"WELL, Kipp was still in the locker room—you know he takes all day to get dressed with his dorky T-shirt of the day."

"That's it?" Mom is about to roll her eyes but stops.

"Well, I wanted to wander on this floor to remember things about Hong Kong. Teachers make us write down stuff about our summer the second we walk into the classroom."

Silence. "And?"

"I promised to remember my impressions for Dad who's all alone now."

Mom morphs from upset to quiet. "Look, Ellie, I'll buy your explanation this time. But you have got to stick close to Kipp. If anything happened to either of you, you can't imagine—so toe the line here."

I bite my lip, wishing I could crawl away to the harbor. "I'll try harder."

We pick up little brother where I try talking to him alone. "Hey, I didn't mean what I said about you not helping Dad." My *Little Brothers for Dummies* manual drills older siblings to take the good with the bad.

"Sorry, El, do-over? Work together?" He slaps elbows with me.

I describe the limo scene to him. "Gerard, the CEO, is supposed to be ridiculously rich. But he still takes his daughter to the Y pool like Dad takes us. Did I tell you he also draws like him? I even have a nickname for him—The Sketcher," I say. "But I still don't get why the Black Turtle Group wants to take over Avabrand. Let's think about this."

We head outdoors where I flip on my happy face. "So, Mom, how was the water? I've never seen you actually in an indoor pool. You're always on the spectator decks when Kipp and I have swim lessons."

She grumbles, "I sure couldn't get in a good workout. Everyone here does breaststroke, bobbing along like turtles."

"Uh, don't you always say different strokes for different folks?" asks Kipp who raises his eyebrows at me.

"You're excellent at selectively remembering my words. It's true I'm used to faster laps doing freestyle."

"What? I never knew you could do serious laps like real swimmers," I say.

Mom chuckles. "And guess what? For circle swim, some of them started on the left side of the lanes, like cars. I messed up and almost collided with another person."

"Did you notice anything about the other swimmers? Did anyone want to talk to you, tap your arm, that kind of thing?" I'm pretty worried.

"Ellie, please stop shouting."

"Was I? My bad."

"Who'd want to address me in the pool, for heaven's sake? A lap swimmer's goal is to keep going without bumping into anyone. Why are you asking?" She narrows her eyes and pauses for me to continue.

I cross my fingers behind me. "I might try out for the middle-school swim team. Which is better— freestyle or breaststroke?"

Mom laughs and says she doesn't know.

Little brother gives me a high-five. "Whoo hoo— you'll be a two-sport athlete."

I whisper to Kipp, "I was kinda kidding with her, but here's a bet. I'll seriously consider it if we can help dad get his company back."

"Deal."

Mom rushes us along. "One good thing about being away from home is eating out every day. I hate planning every meal."

"Plan what? You order takeout almost every day. How come you don't like to cook?" I ask.

"Well, it all started when I received a famous cookbook after I married your dad." She gulps. "Ready for this? The first recipe had some bizarre instructions. I was supposed to grab a chicken and break its head with a blunt instrument. After that, I never recovered."

"Ewww, no wonder. You did the right thing, Mom." I pat her shoulder. "Wait, where are we going?"

"The friend you asked about finally contacted me. Since we're at the Y, she said to meet her next door for lunch." She leads the three of us up the driveway of the Peninsula Hotel that all the brochures describe as legendary.

"Lookit—millions of Rolls-Royces and chauffeurs with gloved hands," Kipp says as we stare at them rubbing off imaginary specks off glistening metal before going in the hotel.

I gaze around in the main lobby. "Wow, this sure is fancy." I put my hair up in a ponytail with Kipp's sports wristband that says GOTTA WANT IT TO WIN IT. And brush down my khaki shorts and top.

"Would you look at these fancy petite tables and elegant stuffed chairs," murmurs Mom under her breath. She smears on a little lip gloss and straightens her slightly damp hair and blouse. "Fake it till I make it. How do I look, Ellie?"

"Good—that dark blue-and-black color looks so nice on you," I say, even though she's worn it zillions of times. We're always, always disagreeing about what color something is. Mom's older and sees and hears things differently than me.

"Thanks, but it's blue and gold." She thinks I need a science class do-over. Her eyes zero in on Kipp's T-shirt. "Do you have a 'Your mom might see you on TV' nice top in your backpack?"

"So, you're saying I'm a walking fashion disaster? It's not like I'll be on TV doing a pizza commercial here." He shrugs and raises his pumped fist. "Anyhow, no one outpizzas the—"

"Stop, please! I'm going to curb your excess

screen time when we get home. And get a better lock for the TV cabinet and put more filters on the Internet." Mom mutters on for a while. "We're a little early, but my friend should be here any minute." She asks us to be quiet and sit.

We can't. "Kipp and I are going to peek downstairs for a few minutes. Be right back."

As we break away, I tell him I'm worried Mr. Han is too busy or absent-minded and unreachable for the rest of our trip. "I wish I knew what I'm doing wrong. I'm still trying to figure out the rest of his note to me."

"Lighten up, and surprise, the answer will appear."

"My goal is to try and get mom's friend alone. What a relief if she knows something about the Black Turtle Group." I wrinkle my nose. "I wonder if I'm not getting anywhere because I'm overanalytical. Or, am I overanalytical because I'm not getting anywhere?"

"Yup. Come on, I wanna shop," Kipp says while pointing to the sign at the end of the hallway—Peninsula Arcade. He knows how to sniff out every shopping place.

"Seriously? Fine, but first, I need to relax."

Without parents around, I give him my deluxe hair toss. First, I roll my eyes and after getting rid of my ponytail, I put up my hair at the top of my head and shake it until it all comes down.

Kipp stares at me, so I tell him Cat and I do that all the time. "I could teach your friend Wynnie—it really calms me down."

"She would hate that silly hair trick. She's not that kind of girl."

"How would you know," I ask, kinda smirking.

Kipp turns all red and immediately clams up. He drags me down the steps to the lower level, poking his nose in each store with his wad of money. But he turns away each time. After complaining about the prices, he nudges my arms into a waiting elevator.

"What? Only one baby flight of stairs up, and you call yourself an athlete?" I tease him. "Oh, I get it— you want to hit the floor buttons."

"Yeah, that's why I came to Hong Kong."

And I'm soooo glad he did.

The elevator panel shows the eighth floor with the letter P next to it, and it can't be the parking garage. The YMCA isn't the only place in town with a pool. As in *alive with swimmers*, Mr. Han's line on his note.

I gulp and press the button, pretending we're hotel guests. "If you don't snitch we went to the upper floors, I won't snitch you looked in the expensive stores."

We creep down the eighth-floor hallway. The mile-high carpet makes me stumble, so my loose sneakers almost fall off. At the outer entrance to the guest pool, we don't see anyone, but the door is ajar. Kipp and I step in.

In front of us, beyond the glass windows, is the clearest, most incredible, best-best pool I've ever seen—a crystal mirror of the harbor. The Y pools next door are great, but this one is ridiculous and belongs in a Roman villa.

"Hello, did you forget your room card key?" asks an attendant with soft pinkish cheeks as she enters from another door.

"We were at your shopping arcade, and we love this great view, and we might stay here in the future," says Kipp. "Please, please, can we go in?"

"I'm afraid not as you are not overnight hotel guests." She talks slowly, smiling, as if she wished she could break the rules for us.

"Oh, um, do local people who are kinda rich ever use the pool regularly with a guest pass or special privileges?" I ask.

The attendant shakes her head. "I do not believe so."

Great. Another dead end. "That awesome view with those tiny boats zipping across the harbor—it must be breathtaking at night."

"Yes, those and the ferries are wonderful. If you are tourists and wish to see dazzling boats at night, another place is Aberdeen." She turns and vanishes through another door.

Vessels by the sea. Nighttime glimmers. Mr. Han's got this thing about water. Who knows what it means, but I remember Dad saying to go with what info you can get. He'd never guess I'm trying to help him.

"Kipp, the guesthouse has sightseeing buses with one to Aberdeen. I think it also goes to the Stanley Market and the Peak," I say and then shake his shoulder. "Oops, I forgot, Mom's friend must have arrived by now. We've got to hurry."

We run down the hall and back into the elevator, where he pushes the button. When the door opens, I say, "This isn't the lobby—I think it's what the British call the first floor. But it's the second floor to Americans. Wait, the stairs are up ahead."

We scamper down the hallway. Approaching the top of the stairway, I trip slightly and lose my triple-

A-size sneaker that rolls down the steps. Kipp makes a leaping dive to get it.

But when his foot kicks back to mine, my legs buckle. We both tumble down the grand staircase of the Peninsula Hotel.

16

EAT, DRINK, TAP FINGERS

I THOUGHT the thick carpet was the enemy when I stumbled. Now Kipp and I have a friend. That and our backpacks protect us from getting hurt.

Thump. Thump. Thummmppp.

I barely swerve in time to avoid the jumbo urns with tall ferns on the side of the staircase. Kipp and I both land on the shiny floor in the main lobby. I'm on my back, facing the octagonal patterns on the ceiling.

People sitting or walking through stop what they're doing. Hotel employees run up to us, but we wave them away. Mom runs up and hugs us, making sure we're not hurt while I put on my shoe. She introduces us to the woman behind her wearing a tan jacket over a silky magenta dress.

"Hello, are you two all right?" Ms. Tang's eyes scan our arms and legs like a parent with a waiting stretcher.

"Yeah, we're fine. Boy, what a fun staircase," says Kipp, avoiding Mom's eyes.

Ms. Tang flashes a favorite-aunt type of smile that I like. "Welcome to Hong Kong. How nice to meet you, Elizabeth—you're almost as tall as your mother. Kipp, you too." Her English sounds crisp, like the TV broadcasters here. "How was your swim at the YMCA?"

"Oh, uh, it was kind of splashy." I cringe, thinking back to Kipp's cannonball and how it messed up my talk with Gerard.

"I'd love to have you be my guests for a late lunch. The hotel's British afternoon tea will start shortly," says Ms. Tang. While standing in line, she teaches Kipp and me how to count in Cantonese and tells us not to worry about the pronunciation tones.

We can't quite grasp the words. Ms. Tang suggests we think of a short flight of steps and learn the words in two batches. Within minutes we've got a sing-songy rhythm—*yat, yi, saam, sei, ng* for one to five. Then *luk, cat, baat, gau, sap* for six to ten. The numbers sound completely different from what I learned in Mandarin Chinese.

Kipp says, "Guess what—when I count to ten slowly in Spanish, my dog Frankie knows I'm upset at her." He gets all huffy when Mom says certain kids react the same way when she counts to ten in English.

"Speaking of Cantonese, does *baak nin* mean anything?" I try spelling it out for her. Mr. Han included that in his scribbles at the museum, and I have no idea why.

"It means one hundred years," says Ms. Tang, just as a train rumbles from Kipp's stomach. She shakes her head. "This queue is too long. Let's try another place."

Kipp jabs my arm and whispers, "Hey word nerd, why did she say Q—like pool cues?"

"Are you talking to me? I'm a word *enthusiast*, remember?" I flash my best dorky grin. "For your information, the word q-u-e-u-e means a line of people."

Ms. Tang overhears us and says, "Nice explanation, Elizabeth. Another meaning of queue was the long braid worn by men during the Qing Dynasty."

"Oh, that's right—we saw pictures of them at the history museum. And please call me Ellie." I smile at her, and she smiles back.

Kipp leads us toward the grand staircase, but

Mom shakes her head and has a whispered fight with him.

Ms. Tang has another suggestion. "Why don't we take the lift to the first floor for some dim sum?"

Upstairs, since our table's not ready, we wait outside the restaurant for a few minutes. Kipp practices saying, "Attention all diners, would Ms. Tang's party of four please come in."

"Yeah, yeah. Keep that up—no one will listen to you." I tease him as we head into the elegant dining room. I've got a thousand questions to ask Mom's friend and make sure I'm sitting next to her.

The restaurant seriously rivals the palaces of emperors and empresses from some of China's ancient dynasties. High up, we see stained-glass types of windows. Mom loves the huge pillars with bold Chinese calligraphy and says she wishes she could read it.

Kipp shows off by shaking out the starched napkin before placing it on his lap.

When our food arrives, I prove readers are eaters. That's how readers become leaders. Duhh. I gobble down every bit of shrimp rice rolls and dumplings, my favorites. I've eaten them in the Los Angeles Chinatown a few times a year, but the food here is what I'd call a banquet.

Except I lose my grip. Same slippery chopsticks here like the guesthouse dining room. With a flick of the ivory, my plump dumpling skids off high and lands without a ripple on the cleanest carpet I've ever seen. Kipp's eyes light up. He's the one who gobbled up my meat bun off the floor yesterday.

I kick his shoe, sort of hard, under the table with a warning. "Don't even think about it."

"What'd you do that for?" mumbles Kipp, making a face at me. Instead of picking up the dumpling, he accidentally kicks it under the table.

"Great foot skills," I whisper and yank his shoulder down for a quick meeting under the table-cloth. "Pssst—don't forget Mr. Han's latest notes to me, if you see a chance to bring something up."

Since baak nin
alive with swimmers
glittering sights and
nighttime glimmers

"Hey, kids, anything interesting under the table?" Mom asks, her face peering at us.

Great—now it's a family convention. "Uh, Kipp thought he lost something." As I get back up, I grip the edge of Ms. Tang's chair with my hand and mess up her elegant jacket. Something flutters to the floor. "Oh, your card must have dropped out."

The travel brochures say many people in Hong Kong have an English name and a Chinese name. One side of the card has all Chinese characters. The other side has her English name, Elizabeth Tang, and some phone numbers with the name of a company.

"Oh, that's all right, you keep it. I'm sorry, that might be dirty—here's another one."

She's a clean freak like me. I push the card deep into the back pocket of my khaki shorts. "Have you always worked at that company?"

"Yes, it's a small one I own. We research and make educational toys for children. Here, I have a sample in my bag," she says and hands me a colorful gadget to make different shapes.

Mom says, "You're always on the road, it seems. It must be tough doing your own marketing and promotional work."

"I'll admit it's hard to keep my schedule straight these days."

"I like the way you say *schedule*," says Kipp as Mom beams. "It sounds like the word without the letter *c*."

Ms. Tang says, "We also add this funny *u* in some

words, but they're silent. Certain words, such as *colour* and *harbour,* are different from American spellings."

"Yeah, as in Victoria Harbour over there," I say and point to the harbor named after Queen Victoria.

"Don't you mean that way?" Kipp asks, pointing the other way. He must have been born with a GPS and Google maps and a compass in his head. Like he knows how to figure out directions inside a building when I can't do it outside of this hotel. Sheesh.

I ask, "By the way, Ms. Tang, do you know how the Peninsula got its name and when it was built?"

"The name is from its location at the tip of the Kowloon peninsula, where I believe they built it in the late 1920s." She puts down her chopsticks and says to Mom, "Your kids sure ask interesting questions."

So, this hotel's been around for almost a hundred years. Kipp and I should have looked around more by the pool area. Why, oh, why do I think of these things afterward?

"Ms. Tang, this might be a dumb question, but what's your favorite sport?" he asks.

I want to place a halo on his head.

"There's no such thing as a dumb question. I love swimming," she says, chuckling.

Kipp flicks his eyes at me before he asks her, "Where do you swim here?"

He's the best brother in the world.

"Growing up, I went to Turtle Cove Beach in the southern part of Hong Kong Island."

"Oh, do people still swim there?" I ask. Like why does this reptile keep popping up?

"I'm uncertain since it's been a while. Speaking of swimming, that's how I indirectly met your mom. I was coming out of the pool locker room and saw her at the indoor track." Ms. Tang smiles and says, "One of her sneakers slipped off, but she picked it up and kept on running. She was in such a rush she pulled it on while hopping on one foot."

Mom laughs. "Running into someone is one sure way to make friends."

"You—on a track?" Kipp leans back and falls out of his chair, taking with him some chopsticks and spoons and forks but not the entire tablecloth. Mom gasps while restaurant servers rush up and hustle him back on his seat, fussing over him as if he's in a high chair.

Ms. Tang makes sure he's all right before saying, "Studying in your country, I felt happy meeting a person with Chinese heritage, even though she was mostly American." She picks up her cup and says, "Oh, this is cold already."

Kipp follows her instructions on opening the top of the teapot lid. After a server magically takes it away and returns with a pot of hot jasmine tea, she says, "Now, the way we show our appreciation is by tapping our fingers like this."

"You mean that's legit here? Some teachers hate that." He laughs in a way that makes Mom wince. Maybe she's thinking he's not an angel at school.

"Let me tell you about an interesting legend behind tapping fingers." Ms. Tang continues, "A disguised emperor traveled throughout his kingdom to observe the people."

She tells us one time he poured tea for a servant who was amazed at this honor. However, he couldn't say thank-you for fear of giving the emperor away. "Instead, the servant bent his three fingers, symbolizing the head and two arms, to express his gratitude for the honor. Today tapping fingers is done to silently thank the person who pours your tea."

Kipp leans forward and yells, "Shut up!"

Mom freezes.

Ms. Tang's eyes widen as she almost drops her teacup.

17

LITTLE BROTHERS

"It means awesome," I say, shaking my head at Kipp. If our parents don't have a clue about certain slang, then that goes double for other people, especially those in other countries.

Kipp says how much he loves the story while his face and neck are trying to figure out if they should stay red. We all laugh, and Mom sits back in her seat and thaws.

Ms. Tang says, "Oh, my ride is coming soon, so please let me take a picture of you three." Before they say goodbye, she and mom hug each other and chat about how her company has struggled at times.

Sheesh. If she leaves now, I'm screwed. I whisper to Kipp, "Can you go shopping with Mom and stay with her? I've gotta talk to Ms. Tang alone."

"Umm." Kipp hesitates like he wants to be in on the action.

I repeat a line from an adventure movie, "This isn't a good day for *umm*."

"OK, you got it, boss." He whisks Mom away, saying he wants her opinion on a store down at the shopping arcade.

"Here, I'll wait with you before your ride comes." I walk with Ms. Tang toward a tall arched window by the front entrance. "Mom said you recommended Mr. Han. Did you know he was the volunteer teacher of my Chinese heritage class? I learned sooo much from him."

"She mentioned searching for a class—I'm glad it all worked out. Walter Han is an acquaintance. I heard he recently returned to Hong Kong and is terrifically busy with additional volunteer work. That's on top of his day job."

Walter Han. In LA, he mentioned his baseball idol was Walter Johnson, the MLB player who said you can't hit what you can't see. So, they share the same first name. Duhh.

"Oh. What's that job?" I ask.

"He's the chairperson of the board of directors for a company he started with his brother Gerard, the CEO."

I stagger and almost drop to the floor. Two brothers who founded a company. I remember reading the article from the guesthouse media room about BTG. But I couldn't read the Chinese. "What's that company?" As if I didn't already know.

"An unusually private one called the Black Turtle Group. They have various subsidiaries, even a cab company." She peers out the window for her ride.

When I met with Mr. Han in Los Angeles, he seemed distracted big time. At the history museum, he was sad. And his brother Gerard, not exactly friendly, looked familiar at the YMCA.

"Is Mr. Walter the older brother?" I ask.

"That's right, the practical one who likes working in the background anonymously."

"Like your story of the disguised emperor who visited his empire?"

Ms. Tang laughs and nods. "I'm not sure if these conglomerates actually have empires, but in some respects, you may be right."

"Does the CEO act like his brother, Mr. Han?" I glance up and want to scream.

Mom and Kipp are heading across the lobby to us—way too early. I try to catch his eye to take another hike. Please, not another catastrophe like at the Y pool.

Softball has thousands of signals, but who can think of any? Unless, wait. He might remember my deluxe hair toss at the shopping arcade. I put up all my hair on my head, shake it all down, and flick my head. Out of the corner of my eye, my little brother, teammate extraordinaire, does a U-turn with Mom. I swear he winked at me first.

Ms. Tang tries to hide a smile and pretends not to notice my messy hair. "I believe the brother loves betting on riskier things and is quite stubborn. I know little about him."

"So is Gerard the top, top boss? Or, could the real boss be someone named Sofie?" That's the name he mentioned to the woman by the pool before my flops hit his leg.

"It's possible outsiders can play an influential role."

What am I going to do? I can't admit I met Mr. Han briefly at the museum, or she might tell Mom. And although I met Gerard, that didn't pan out. "Do you know where Mr. Han's volunteer work is?"

When she looks at me with a big question mark, I say, "He said if any of his students visit Hong Kong, we should look him up."

"I heard he's very private. If he returned a short while ago, he might be busy, Ellie, and I wouldn't want you to get your hopes up." She peers out the window and gets ready to leave. "There's my ride. It was wonderful meeting you."

"Me, too. Wait, Ms. Tang, can you think how I can contact him? I have his email, but he's so absent-minded he doesn't check often. I wish I had his cell number."

She hesitates before saying, "I'll try, but I'm not altogether optimistic. I can try to get his number from friends of friends. How's that? Why don't you call me tomorrow?"

"Oh, and I forgot, is a trip to Aberdeen worth it? The tour also goes to the Stanley Market and the Peak."

"Oh, absolutely. Such a gorgeous harbor, where you'll see how some local people live. The Stanley Market has great shopping bargains, and the views from the Peak are magnificent."

That's what I call something for everyone. "I can't wait to go." I've got higher stakes than sightseeing, though.

Ms. Tang says, "Although I live here, I dislike the heavy rain and humidity, but tomorrow will be sunny, so have fun. It's nice to know we have much in common." She rushes out before I can ask what she means.

I join Mom and my little brother on a bus back to Central where he and I sit together.

After a few minutes, Kipp squeals, "Lookit on the sidewalk, a golden retriever. And that person over there has a poodle and a terrier." His grin disappears. "I miss Frankie."

"I miss her, too. But, sometimes she's so not into me." I shake my head.

He frowns and shifts his eyes back and forth. "Like you really walk her a lot. How come you don't like picking up her poop?"

"You wouldn't either if you plowed into Frankie's clump and it smeared all over your hands and elbows. I fell right on it when my bike skidded," I say, shuddering. "Cleaning it up was awful. On my bike, my clothes, and me. That's why." One whiff, and I've never forgotten the smell of those messy meadow muffins.

"Yeah, but at least she's not that snarky anymore. Frankie had a blast in her behavior class." He says proudly, "She got third prize."

I remember she came home as Francesca from the Humane Society. When Kipp signed up for the class, it had only ten spaces to register her name. That's how she became Frankie Wei. Pets in our family take Mom's last name.

"Yup, she's got that new swagger. But wait, didn't Dad say only three dogs were in that class?" I narrow my eyes at him.

"Details, details." Kipp shrugs. "I hope she's getting along now with Russ. He likes dogs and doesn't mind picking up her poop."

"Excuse me—who?" I twist my head to see if I've heard correctly, hearing a name that sounds out of place in Hong Kong. "I thought Wynnie was walking her."

"She's got soccer and math camps this week at the Y. Russ is walking Frankie when Dad's at work."

"Oh." I. Need. To. Calm. Down. I never dreamed Kipp knows him. I'd die if my little brother knows I like our pet sitter.

Russ and I hang around with the same friends. One day he became more special, and I don't know how it all started. Once in math class, he glanced over at me, sitting a few seats behind the front row. A few minutes later when he did it again, my head went down. When I peeked at him, he pretended not to notice. The rest of the day, nothing. The next day, same thing.

Frankie has all the luck. When I return, if she could talk, I hope she'll tell me about all her walks, every glance, every romantic bow-wow in any language, any onomatopoeia.

After we get off the bus, Kipp tears down the steep road like he does this every day. He twirls and prances, holding an imaginary lacrosse stick. "Watch me. I catch a pass from the face-off guy, race down the field, and cradle the ball while splitting two defenders. Seeing an opening, I shoot it into the net."

"Quit hotdogging—my quads are burning." Granddad once said that walking the Great Wall in northern China wasn't that easy with steep inclines and craggy, uneven steps. Guess I won't go there anytime soon.

"Kipp, be careful you don't fall. And slow down, kids," says Mom, but she's taking the slope faster than us. That's her, a swimmer and a runner. "Need a hand?"

"No offense, but I always thought you were a couch slouch," I say, giggling. "I never knew why you posted that 'Fitness Guide for Dummies' article on the kitchen bulletin board."

"Things aren't always what they seem."

"Funny—Dad said that to me, too." On a normal day, Mom and I would never be talking like this. But on this trip away from home, I like finding out new things about her. "Didn't you say that exhaling longer than inhaling gives you energy?"

"That's right. Do the most strenuous activity on the exhaling part." She passes Kipp.

"You go on ahead—I'll be there soon." I slow to a crawl and when I arrive at the guesthouse, find my way to the media room. I send out a quick email, an important one.

Dear Mr. Han, I'm sure I saw Gerard at the YMCA. But I struck out before we talked much. Is there any other place else I could meet him? I need your help.

Your student, Ellie.

What's killing me is why Mr. Han didn't tell me his brother is the CEO of Black Turtle. Twice he could have told me. Unless he didn't know what was going on about Dad's company. Maybe he found out about the takeover the same time we talked in LA. He was surprised and upset about something as we were leaving.

Gerard is his little brother. If Kipp were up to something big, I might have done the same thing. I'd feel crappy if I didn't know what was going on.

Fingering the outline of my family memories box in my backpack calms me down.

I trust Mr. Han.

Walter Han.

DAY FOUR

18

STOP AND SHOP

"Why didn't Mr. Han answer you?" Kipp asks the next morning in the media room.

I let out a deep breath. "As if I know. So, we'll have to work with what we've got. He warned me he'd be busy, and I'll bet he'll forget to send me his new cell number. Maybe Ms. Tang can get it."

"Yeah, 'cause the world revolves around us." In a minute, he brightens up. "I'll have to tell Frankie about the other dogs I saw here."

"Uh, now how did you say you know Russ?" I'm hoping my voice sounds chill.

"Lacrosse bro. Travel team." Kipp clams up.

"Oh, that's nice." I still can't believe my brother knows the guy I want to know better. "Since when were you on a travel team?"

"Who said I was? You have to be really good. I watched the middle school guys try out—they're so much better than my school team." Kipp spits out, "You got it?"

Wow! So, Kipp's worried he's not as good as he thinks he is. "Kinda touchy, aren't you?" I say. I think he's the best in sports. But maybe he's not a big athlete, head of the pack and everything. "Anyhow, we'll be home soon to get back on our regular sports schedules."

Except we've got this tiny thing to do now. Help Dad!

When Mom returns from her morning workshop, the three of us board the sightseeing bus. At the first stop, we get off and stretch our legs where a few clouds hang overhead on a slightly sunny day. I pat my skin that's literally jumping up and down from the cool harbor breeze.

The tour guide gives bits and pieces of history. "Aberdeen, like the Stanley Market, is named after a British aristocrat. They created a permanent trading outpost right near here."

I ask, "Ma'am, when was that?"

"In the mid-1800s under British sovereignty," she replies, after looking on her clipboard. She straightens her name tag on her crisp, white blouse.

So, Aberdeen's been here over a hundred years. This might be the place Mr. Han was talking about when he wrote *since baak nin* in his scribbles to me. Ms. Tang said it means one hundred years in Cantonese. Like I know what any of this means yet.

Kipp points to boats of every kind in the aquamarine harbor. "Aren't those real sampans over there?"

The tour guide explains that many boat dwellers still live on them, fishing and giving sightseeing tours. "Their lives and activities are different from the typical tourist sights."

Mom says, "What a contrast after seeing the ultra-luxury cars at the Peninsula Hotel."

"Guess what, we saw a sampan exhibit at the museum. And there was a man on the deck," Kipp says to the tour guide as he starts doodling by the railing near the water.

She tells him politely to be careful and asks in a gentle voice, "Which museum was it?"

Suddenly he can't remember after I give him the big-sister glare. To make sure, I swish my fingers across my neck, hoping he picks up the hint to not squeal. If Mr. Motormouth blabs all over Hong Kong about our mission, we might get nowhere.

Mom stares at Kipp and me. "What was that all about, Ellie?"

"Nothing, nothing—we saw some lifelike mannequins at the history museum." Before she can say anything further, I ask to use her cell to call Ms. Tang. "She said I could follow up if I have any questions." When she agrees, I walk away from the group.

Ring-ringgg, ring-ringgg. Hong Kong sure has a funny ringtone.

A person answers first in Cantonese and then in English. "Tang Learning Express, may I help you?"

After a minute, Ms. Tang gets on the line. "Elizabeth, er Ellie, hello. I was delighted to meet you yesterday."

"Me, too, and I love the sample toy you gave me. Did you find out anything about my teacher?"

"All I could do was contact a mutual acquaintance of Walter Han. I left a message saying you'd be at the Stanley Market and Victoria Peak today. I included your mom's cell number."

Sheesh, what if he calls and Mom answers? "We're going to go to those places soon. Thank you so much, Ms. Tang. So, I guess he's unavailable, huh?"

"He's supposed to be the busiest man on earth

since returning here. Hope for the best, Ellie. Don't worry."

I keep hearing those two words, but I'm not afraid now. "Uh, Ms. Tang? Please don't tell Mom about Mr. Han's background and company. I'm trying to help Dad with a little thing."

"That's fine. But I wouldn't want you struggling here."

"Could I ask you something else? Um, how do you say *help me* in Cantonese?"

"You mean, for example, you need suggestions on a menu?" Ms. Tang chuckles.

"No, uh, in case an emergency comes up." I don't hear anything on the other end for a while.

"Ellie, is everything all right?"

"Yeah, nothing's wrong. But, what if I saw someone who needed help on the street or subway stop?"

"Oh, right. You'd say *gau meng ah,* but only for actual emergencies."

"Thank you, Ms. Tang." I feel so good knowing that phrase.

I discuss my call with Kipp when he points to the water. "Excuse me, please, what's that over there?"

The tour guide gets all excited. "That is a floating seafood restaurant. It's truly gorgeous at night when glittery lights outline the shape of the boat and brighten up the harbor." She walks around to get people back on the bus.

Glittering sights. Nighttime glimmers. I wish I knew what it all means.

———

KIPP DROOLS as he enters a shopping heaven. I'm not into buying things, but he fits right in.

Scads of shoppers walk among the shops and stalls among a gazillion things for sale. Everything blends together—splashy red, yellow, and blue pinwheel colors spinning around us.

Mom and many other sightseers want to buy linen. "Stick by my side, kids."

"Kipp's the only kid here. Can we look for gifts by ourselves? This place is like a mall, so we can't get lost." I figure this is about the only way she'll give me her cell again.

"Absolutely not. This area is too busy."

OK, Plan B. I make sure the other people can hear me. "Mom, please, I have to get a gift for Cat, and I can't do that while you're shopping for linen."

Some of the grown-ups nod like they understand, but Mom insists, "Please don't argue with me, Ellie."

"I've got to go," interrupts Kipp.

"I asked you to stay with me." Mom hisses softly but with a smile on her face.

"But I really have to go." He twists his legs together and clutches his hands in front of his shorts. If he has an accident, she'll be labeled as a failed potty trainer at the Stanley Market.

And she knows it. Mom widens her eyes and gulps. "All right, find the restroom and catch up with us." She apologizes to the others while handing over her cell and the number of the tour guide in case we need to contact her. "I want you two back in ten minutes, tops, and remind him to you-know-what, please."

With an inner GPS, you can go places. Kipp finds the restroom in zero seconds.

As I'm waiting for him, the cell rings. I jump up, startled. Like when did my wishes ever come true. "Uh, hello?"

"Ellie, is that you? I've been meaning to touch base but only have a few seconds."

"Oh, Mr. Han, am I ever so glad you called. I'm at the Stanley Market now and stuck. I can't figure out how to contact Gerard. We're only here tomorrow and leaving the next day." I practically moan and groan.

"Here, why don't we do this? Locate a particular small shop near the center of the market that sells crafts and things." He gives me some specific instructions on the location. "Pick up a T-shirt and ask for a colorful bag. Keep that bag visible at the Market and at the Peak."

"But, why?"

"I've got someone coming in to talk to me now, so bye for now and take care of yourself. Remember what I told you before. Now is not the time to give up. When you believe in yourself, things will open up," he says in a calm voice.

"Thank you. And oh, Mr. Han—will I see you again?" I've got a thousand unanswered questions.

But he's already hung up.

As Kipp comes out of the restroom, I say. "So, you flushed, right?"

"Stop being such a control freak."

After I inwardly roll my eyes, I tell him what happened. "We've got to find the shop that Mr. Han told me about. I wish he wasn't always super busy. And I still have to figure out the meaning of his messages. Why, oh why, are they so vague?"

We find the place where a motherly type of

shopkeeper pulls me in as if she's expecting me. With a shy smile, she places a black T-shirt in my hands. I stare and rub my fingers over the turquoise square in the center with its shimmery peach silk and tiny black designs.

The shopkeeper won't take my money. She places the shirt in a giant, orange neon bag and insists I carry it over my shoulders. All this happens so fast that before I can even thank her, she shoos us out the door.

As Kipp and I make our way back to Mom, he asks, "What kind of gift could I get for someone who loves sports and dogs?" He mumbles one long, jumbled word under his breath. "Andthisperson-likesnumbers."

Hmmm, who does he know that likes sports and dogs and numbers? "Look, we can't stop and shop now. But, you say it's for a girl who likes math? How about a calculator?"

"I didn't say who it was for. And I don't want this person to think that I like her. You know, like but not like-like. And I'm not loaded."

"Lots of gifts don't cost a ton here." He's wasting my time. He and Wynnie were whispering about some *GF* at our house before our trip. Maybe she's officially his girlfriend. "Wanna talk about it?"

"Talk about what?" Kipp shrugs, like I'm in his face.

"Honestly, I'm only trying to help." In front of me, I see a perfect gift for Cat in a shop window. "Wait right here, would you. Or, let's go in together. No? Then, get lost."

I rush in to pick up and pay for the gift. Then my goose bumps start.

Too quiet.

I race up and down the aisles like a flashlight stumbling around in the dark. "Kipp?" No answer. I exhale and try again. "Can't you take a joke? Come on out—I give up."

No kid with dimples pops up.

I cup my hands around my mouth and yell, "Oh, Kiiipppp. I'm going to try out for lacrosse."

19

MISSING YOU

NOTHING. If Kipp is gone, I don't know what'd I do. He's the best brother. Ever.

Have you ever heard a washer spin cycle that's stuck? That's me. Why is this happening?

I retrace my steps back to the restroom. It can be impossible when I don't always pay attention to where I've been. The first shop is kinda familiar, but not this watch store. The electronics place looks new. Nope. Same for the jewelry store and the handbags stall.

No Kipp.

I rush around some more aisles, trying not to panic. At the next fork, a long queue forms in front of a shop with a large sign saying it's going out of business. It's an outlet store for a company in

Kowloon and above it are a few lines of Chinese characters.

A sizeable crowd of people are bummed out with worried faces. A few of them are talking in English.

"They said our jobs would be safe."

"My father has been with this company forever."

As I'm walking past, the woman from the guest-house reception office sees me, startled. She explains, "I'm trying to help my neighbor here pick up her things. That Black Turtle Group we talked about announced her company is being taken over." She points to a woman nearby.

I get it. This must be that local company mentioned by the BBC news on the plane. It was supposed to be in a hostile takeover by the Black Turtle Group. Dad's company would be next.

"I hope your neighbor gets another job soon. Can I help with anything?" I ask.

"No, Miss. Are you by yourself—where's your family?"

I start blubbering. "Actually, I was searching for my brother. He's lost."

"Go, go—up ahead, beyond that corner. You'll see the Information Booth on your right. Good luck," she calls out as I sprint away.

"Thanks, and tell your neighbor I hope everything works out," I yell out and run.

At the booth, I cry out to the attendant, "Excuse me, how do I report a lost person?"

Taking out her pen and paper, she asks me to describe him.

"Short brown hair. Baseball cap, usually worn backwards. Almost five feet." I sniffle.

The woman scowls at me and tilts her head. "In centimeters?"

"Uh, I'm unsure, but he's about half a head shorter than me." I point to my ear. "And he's wearing a T-shirt."

"What color is it, and does it have a design?"

Sheesh. "I don't remember. Does it matter? You see, he changes a couple of times a day 'cause he's got hundreds of freaking T-shirts."

"Freaking? What does that mean?"

Ohhhhhh. I start to blubber again.

A man who's in the queue behind me calls out to the attendant. He points to a nearby exit and tells us a young boy with brown hair got on a bus by himself minutes ago. I tear out of the shopping area in time to see a bus rumbling down the street.

The sign on the back says "Aberdeen."

Kipp, why, oh, why are you doing things on your

own—that's not teamwork. I grab a pen from my backpack and jot down the number of the bus and the time it left the stop.

World's biggest klutz loses her little brother. I return and pass another crafts store, cold and lonely as a discarded tea bag. The kind of tea the emperor didn't serve his servant in Ms. Tang's story about tapping fingers.

Now for the hard part.

With unsteady fingers, I pull out Mom's phone and punch in the tour guide's cell number. She doesn't answer. When people are shopping, who picks up? No one. N.O.

If there's a sports god, please, please keep Kipp safe.

"Ahhhhhh—gau meng ah!" I'm so frustrated, I start crying.

Until I hear it.

"Attention, all shoppers. Softball player Elizabeth P., please meet your party at the Information Booth." The announcement over a loudspeaker booms loud and clear.

I know that annoying voice, always talking about sports. I've lived with it for almost ten years.

Flying back to the Information Booth, I almost lose my sneakers again. Next to the attendant is an almost five-foot-tall boy wearing a T-shirt that says UNFINISHED BUSINESS. He holds a microphone and wears a cap dumped backwards on messy brown hair.

I grab his arms and kinda squeeze his shoulders and hug him. "Kipp, where were you?"

"Checking out stuff," he says and smiles. "I found a gift for my, I mean, a friend."

"That's not funny—you were supposed to be right by me. Why did you vanish?"

Words pour out of his mouth like a running faucet. "You were being bossy and saying I had to do this and that. I was right by you, but I'm the attackman. A bunch of defensive midfielders came at me, so I tried for a fast break, but you were gone."

"That literally makes no sense. You're not on a lacrosse field, and you're not charging down the field with the ball." I'm so upset I'm sounding like Mom.

As I walk away, Kipp pretends he's going to prevent me from leaving. Nice try, but I swerve to the left and right and dodge his moves.

"You call that being a good defender? Take it away, Wei," I say.

"You're OK."

"Just OK? Lacrosse must be easy. Now softball, that's a thinking person's game." I giggle.

"El, when you thought I was lost, a bunch of people were talking about swimmers," says Kipp. "I couldn't hear them well, but it was about a hotel right on the water. Not the Peninsula. This one sounds like—"

A herd of people stampede up to us. O.M.G. I totally forgot about the ten-minute limit.

Mom's leading the pack. "Ellie, how could you? Kipp, what happened?"

I thought he was scared. But now, mr. motor-mouth brags about how he was shopping, and it's all about him, blah-blah, kipp, little brother, transportation vice president.

He doesn't deserve capital letters.

First Mom checks him over like he had double arm and knee surgeries. He squirms and wiggles. Then she scolds him big time. "Running off by yourself? You're grounded, Little Mister."

Kipp explained to me once what happens in lacrosse if a player commits a penalty. The team continues with one fewer player, or "man down," until the penalty is lifted.

I cannot afford a man down. I need my little brother.

Pulling Mom off to the side, I whisper, "Sorry, I'm the one who flubbed up. I was kinda distracted buying a gift for Cat and must have left Kipp by accident."

She looks at me like I'm an axe murderer. "That's all fine and good. But a good babysitter never loses sight of the kids. You're grounded, too."

"I'm not his babysitter, so I can't be grounded—it's my vacation. I've got things to do, I mean, more places I want to see." Talk about being unreasonable. And she doesn't know I'm trying to help Dad, her, our family.

"At the Y, we were all together in one building. Here, there are too many little shops and stalls. You definitely crossed the line."

Mom runs back to Kipp. "Stick close to Ellie. When we're back in California, let me think about you carrying one of our cells."

"Not El's old hand-me-down one," he says, whining and flashing those buy-me-a-new-cell dimples. "No wait, any cell is fine. I can't wait to start making those butt dials."

"Mom, are you saying that Kipp gets a cell for free after you bribed me to take that heritage class? And I have to wait until August to get mine? That's so wrong." I glare at her as we board the tour bus. And here I thought we were getting closer on this trip.

"Listen, Ellie. Try to remember I don't do bribes, well, except for the time you boycotted broccoli. Also, when you wouldn't memorize those multiplication tables. And then there was—but anyhow, getting you that cell is an achievement gift," she says and scrunches both hands at her waist. "And why did Kipp say *Elizabeth P.* in his announcement? What's going on?"

"He was joking. Mr. Han calls me that 'cause there were two Elizabeths in the heritage class." I slide into a seat near the front by Kipp while she heads to the rear.

I'll bet he's already forgotten Mom yelled at him. Me? It'll take a long time to get over it.

"Kipp, what were you saying earlier about swimmers near some hotel?" I yawn and feel my eyes drooping.

"Yeah, this one had a name like a continental breakfast or something."

My eyes jerk open like window blinds at home when I twist the wand. "Come to think of it, a hotel called the InterContinental Hong Kong is supposed to be near the Star Ferry Pier. I remember seeing a picture in the travel brochure. Are you sure that's what you heard?"

"Yeah, I'm sure, why?" Kipp's eyes look sleepy as they flicker.

"Today is impossible. But let's definitely go there tomorrow, our last day."

I lean back on the bus seat and close my eyes.

———

AND OPEN them when Kipp says, "Drum roll, please, for the Peak."

That's short for Victoria Peak, the top of the world where everyone comes to visit. It's like the Empire State Building or the Great Wall of China or the Eiffel Tower.

As we get off the bus, Mom eyes my bag I've been trying to hide from her. "Did you buy something at the Stanley Market?"

I gulp and say, "Yeah, remember I bought a gift for Cat in one of the shops?"

"Cute bag. You sure stand out with that orange neon color."

"Cute? Is the fate of the world in my hands cute?" Sheesh.

"There's no need to be melodramatic." She shakes her head at me before buying our tickets.

The queues for the ride up on the Peak Tram are

worse than the lines when a blockbuster movie comes out. All I can do is stand with Kipp and Mom and read a brochure on its history.

So, the tram was built in 1888 and is operated by cables—a funny word called funicular. Back then, wealthy people working below the hills rode the tram to get to their homes high among the hills. Up there, it's not boiling hot in the summers. Before the tram, workers carried people back and forth in portable bamboo chairs up the steep hills. Nope, they sure weren't the fancy sedans used by the bride in the history museum exhibit.

Finally, when it's our turn to board, we hang on for the seven-minute ride up toward the clouds. "Guess what—I read about this Peak Tram Illusion." I explain the high-rise buildings on the right side of the tram will act like they're falling toward the Peak. It's due to the "tilted visual environment" and the leaning back position of the passengers.

"Hey, yo, this is the sickest ride I've ever taken," says Kipp as he hangs on tightly. When we arrive at the top, he snaps his NEVER GIVE UP wristband. "El, do you think it'll rain tomorrow? Look at those cumulus clouds above, like cotton candy. Technically they're pretty, but what if they mess up someone's plans?"

"Exactly what technical thing are you trying to say?" If anything else goes wrong, I don't know what I'd do.

"What if I want to have a picnic or do something secret by the water?"

"What do you mean secret?"

20

UNIQUE PEAK

"Nothing, nothing." Kipp shrugs. "Hey, why do ducks make great detectives?"

"Why?" I'm on to him about changing the subject.

"They always quack the case."

"Wow—your first onomatopoeia—that quacks me up." I try to hug him, but he dodges me while insisting he's not verbal or a word nerd or a word enthusiast.

After lunch as we're walking out past the shops, we see Madame Tussauds, a wax museum that's a branch of the original one in London. It reminds me of what I thought was a fake mannequin standing on the sampan deck at the history museum.

"Mom, could we go in? But wait." I read the

notice by the front entrance. "Of all the luck—it's closed. The date on the sign doesn't even make sense. It's got these November and December dates for what they call quick repairs."

"Here, let me see. No, it's correct. Many places in the world put the day before the month. So these are mid-month days in June," she says.

"Ohhhh—got it. My homework spreadsheet does that when I type in dates."

Kipp and I hustle to the outside viewing area while Mom says she'll catch up. Before we leave, she grins and points two fingers to her eyes and then to us, mouthing the words, "I'm watching you."

Sheesh. It's her way of saying she loves us a lot.

Mr. Han was right about pushing me to see some of Hong Kong, especially this highest point on the island. The late morning fog has blown away, and bits of blue sky peek out as if I'm back home. I love breathing in fresh air like clean jerseys when I first take them out of a hot dryer.

The bird's-eye view of the peninsula is a thousand times better than looking up streets on a cell phone or the Internet. Beyond that, from my map, is the northern part of Hong Kong, what they call the New Territories. Way, way beyond that is northern

China where Granddad came from. I'm closer to him here than when I'm in California.

I think about what Ms. Tang said about Mr. Han and Gerard. The brothers have different ways of doing business. At the history museum, Mr. Han told me they're not talking with each other. And if they're not, how can either help me stop the Black Turtle Group's takeover?

On top of that, Mr. Han had me pick up a T-shirt and bag. That's insane.

I've got to step back and get a different angle on things, like in the Peak Tram Illusion. Only a day and a half left before we leave Hong Kong. Or, as Mr. Han said, two teams are tied at the bottom of the final inning, and I'm the next batter.

My problem is it's not even close to a tied score.

"Lookit, that must be Kowloon. Those buildings over there are near the YMCA and that Peninsula Hotel." Kipp points beyond the teeny-tiny boats and ferries being chased by a faint breeze as they cross the shimmering waves of Victoria Harbour.

I adjust the oversize bag on my shoulder while Kipp grabs the T-shirt inside and pulls it out.

He says, "Sweet. Uh, looks like it's one size fits all —mind if I have it?"

"Here's the thing. Our partnership doesn't

provide uniforms. And do you really need one more to add to your collection? You've become a clotheshorse." I swat him with the orange neon bag. In a sisterly way.

That's when someone who looks like a high school kid in a suit and shades walks straight toward me. He hands me something I've seen many times before. A thickish, cream-colored envelope almost 100 percent cotton. The kind that Mom handles in her work for people who love elegant stationery.

I grab a corner of the stranger's arm while shouting, "Wait, who are you?" He takes off while I stand with my mouth open, watching his disappearing back.

"Hey, stop!" I avoid running into some tourists and run as fast as I can, almost overtaking him. This is not a good time to lose my shoe again. Sheesh.

When the guy takes one backward look at me, his face reminds me of someone being left behind in a school fire drill. He plows right into a noisy tour group that takes up the size of two classrooms. I try like crazy to find him but end up getting stepped on.

I wait five seconds, thinking he'd have to pass me. Except I don't know the layout of this area. All I can do is stay near the Peak Tram, hoping he'll pass me to get on.

Nope. After a long while, he doesn't reappear. So, I stop and rip open his envelope where a name jumps out at me.

"Elizabeth P., kindly meet my daughter and me at the Star Ferry pier in Central in the next half hour. Gerard W. Han."

His Chinese signature has a chop next to it. I learned in heritage class that a chop seal is like a signature. It's the message I've been waiting for.

Kipp runs up. "What'd you do, where'd you go, what'd you see? I never saw you race that fast, although you run like a girl."

"I am a girl." Honestly. Annoyed, I use my headband to push back my hair again.

"Gonna try out for the cross-country team?" Kipp bends his right elbow back and points his left arm upward in the pose of one of the world's fastest runners.

Mom is walking toward us, so I whisper to him that Gerard sent me a note and we've got to leave here like yesterday. I crush the neon bag and T-shirt into my backpack. "Shush, she's back."

"Here you are, Ellie, and where's Kipp? How hard can it be to keep track of two kids?" Mom sighs.

Kipp pops up. "I'm right here. No need to call a search team."

I plunge in. "Since we're done early, how about we go to the pier that's about fifteen minutes away? We'd have to go that way anyhow to take the regular bus back to the guesthouse. The tour bus won't be back for a while."

"I'd love to go, but it's been a long day and I'm exhausted," croaks Mom.

"They say there's a great English bookstore near the pier."

"Who's they? That's too ambiguous for me."

Tilting my head slightly, I beg Kipp with my eyes to back me up. If he does a good job, I might even reconsider providing him with a team uniform. A new T-shirt, of course.

He says, "Uh, I need to get something for someone since we're leaving sometime soon."

"Something, someone, sometime—hmmm, that's what I call precise." Mom shifts her eyes upward. "Wait, bookstore? OK, but make it fast. When I grounded you two, I never dreamed it would be so much more work." She throws her hands up in the air.

Whew—Gerard, here I come.

I don't know if he's reliable. I don't know if he'll appear. I don't know what I'll do if he doesn't.

All I know is that I've got to take risks to get rewards.

AFTER GETTING off the Peak Tram, Mom tucks on her sun hat and marches us out to Garden Road. Eventually we reach Des Voeux Road, where the crowds feel like we're stuck in molasses.

I make plans with Kipp once we're on the footbridge, a wide throughway up above the swarming traffic below. "After we arrive at the bookstore, I'll slip away. Gerard's note said to meet in half an hour, so I have no time to lose."

"How long will you be gone?" asks Kipp.

"Not too long, I hope. After I leave, try to distract Mom so she won't worry. Can we brainstorm on how to deal with Gerard?" I sigh big time. "I wish I could break down an opponent's strategy. What do you call it—cause a turnover during a game?"

"Remember, you said we would not talk about sports in Hong Kong, ever." Kipp smirks. In a brotherly way.

"Yeah, don't remind me what I said at the airport. But now things have changed."

After a minute, he says, "Gonna try out for a fall sport? What about the cross country team?"

I knew it—he's the one who can't stop talking sports 24/7. I pivot to face him. "Seriously? Can you dial in, Kipp?"

He takes off his baseball cap and puts it on again in a different position. "OK, here's the poop. Lots of times players can't figure things out on the field. But our coaches see the big picture. At time-outs, they always tell us how to adjust."

"Softball's different, so what do you do in your team sports?"

"Reset and return to the fundamentals. Quick, Mom's turning around." He and I both smile and wave to her before she continues walking. "And we've got to make attempts, like making those shots on goal. We're sure to make the lacrosse net one of those times."

"That makes sense, kinda like what Babe Ruth is supposed to have said. Every strike brings a player closer to the next home run. No wonder he became so consistent." I've got to be ready. I just have to. If I don't, my whole life will change.

At the bookstore in Exchange Square, I wish I could stop and read what's on shelf after shelf of hard covers and soft covers. There's one I'd die to read now.

But meeting Gerard is why I came. I dawdle until Mom's busy with Kipp and tiptoe around the next corner. Sheesh—she's practically a nose away from me.

"See anything interesting, Ellie?" She picks up a book and flips through the pages.

"Oops, I forgot. While we're here, um, I've got to pick up a ferry schedule at the pier. Be right back."

Mom puts both hands on her waist. "What for? I'm sure those ferries come every few minutes. You can't be scampering about."

"Yeah, but I'm trying to work on a detailed travel report for Dad. I'll need a glossy pamphlet that's the equivalent of beautiful stationery, the kind you salivate over." I go for the close. "Do you really want me to attach a schedule printed on cheap, thin copier paper? That's so gross."

"Here's a better option—we'll all go down together when we're finished here."

"No, Mom, please, let me do this. I promised Dad a super job on my reports. Can't you trust me to go a half block away? I swear I'll be OK, or I'll give up the new cell you promised me."

Kipp shouts, "Over here, Mom, what do you

think about this book? It's got instructions and everything. Perfect for my, uh, any friend."

Mom shifts her eyes back and forth, thinking. One side of the brain eventually wins. "Be right there. Now, Ellie, be very careful and use landmarks like we discussed."

"It's literally next door, so I'll be fine. Don't forget I'm twelve."

"I wish I had you and Kipp in back-to-back cribs, nice and safe."

I let out a deep breath and explode. "Great— that's great! Don't you think I learned to be cautious from you? Be careful crossing the streets. Don't give anyone personal information. Try not to get hurt in sports." I squeeze my fists around the shoulder straps of my backpack. "You wonder why I'm not decisive. And when I do try things by myself, you complain I'm overthinking and have to get my butt off that boat."

"Behind."

"OK. To get my behind off the overanalytical boat."

"This, too, shall pass," she says in a low voice and looks up. "You're right. Here, take my cell. And LOL."

"THAT'S SO NOT FUNNY, MOM."

"What's wrong with saying lots of love?" She's gushing up.

"Ohhhh. LOL to you, too. I'll be back before Kipp blabs about sports again." I turn away from her as I'm gushing up, too.

I walk across the footbridge toward the pier where bluish waves with gold streaks sparkle in the harbor. People scurry back and forth by the ticket windows and the green-and-white ferries. Nearby, I grab a schedule but can't find my black journal, so throw it in my backpack.

When I zip open a compartment to grab my water bottle, the T-shirt from the Stanley Market shop almost drops out. Taking it out, this time the tiny designs in the middle look like turtles forming funny letters. I hold the shirt a foot away from my eyes.

Yup, it's a message. Nope, I can't read it, and I don't need glasses that I know of. At this point, I've got to understand any message, so I pull the tee closer to my eyes.

Freaking T-shirts. Teachers said we wouldn't ever need to know cursive. Now I do.

I've struck out. I kick the dirt. Except it's a cement sidewalk, and my big toe is paying for it. I hop on one foot to shake it out and try to remember the letters in Mom's handy cursive guide. What I learned on the plane didn't exactly stick with me.

That leaves only one thing to do.

I stand against a wall and start twirling my foot starting with the letter A in the Ankle Alphabet. If you know anything about cursive, it means your foot jiggles a little. Or a lot.

People pass me and immediately glance back. Some return. A little crowd gathers, some starting to kind of sway and dance. But wanting me to lead them with my steps. I know the signs. Like the guinea pig leading a dance in the movie my family watched.

The Star Ferry Pier is the perfect place for a flash mob dance.

But no one else is jumping in and waving their arms and shaking their heads and behinds while keeping step with the music. The only song is me humming "ABCD." It's not exactly what I'd call pop music.

Instead of introducing a marriage proposal or another big event, I'm busy figuring out each letter on the T-shirt design. Finally, I've got it—EBONY SEA ANIMAL CONNECTS ALL.

Sheesh. Another funny message from dear old Mr. Han.

I'm no fun, so the small crowd fades away. Two people remain.

One is a little girl who stops swaying, the one from the YMCA pool with the black turtle toy.

The other is a man who walks straight toward me. The Sketcher wears a business suit with a small white hanky in his suit pocket. Lean and mean. His tortoise-like glasses don't hide his piercing eyes.

He towers over me as I stare. In a rumbling voice, he says, "Are you Elizabeth P.?"

I slowly take some steps back and run into a big fat pole in a corner near the ticket office. I'm only brave on the outside. As mom said at the lobby of the Peninsula Hotel, fake it till I make it. I gulp and say, "Yup, that's me."

"I am Gerard, and you must have received my note."

I'm nervous, so I blurt out to my enemy, "Like what is this all about? Why did you send me a message?"

"Please calm down. I will explain in a while."

"And how did you know where I would be today?"

"Acquaintances of mine thought you would likely be at the Peak this afternoon. They mentioned a flashy orange shopping satchel," he says. "I took a risk. By the way, have you perhaps seen—"

The little girl tugs my backpack, making him glance at her.

I kneel down and say, "Hi, I saw you at the YMCA pool. Do you go often?"

Gerard interrupts, "Oh—please forgive me—this is my daughter Sofie. I am babysitting her this week at the office as my wife is away."

Seriously? He's a babysitter like me.

Sofie smiles at me, a little shy. "I take swimming lessons. You helped me get my turtle."

"That's right. Here's something else you can play

with." I give her the toy from Ms. Tang after her dad nods OK.

I want to talk about Avabrand but with so much at stake, I'm shaking. So I do a warm-up. "Wait, are you taking over a company in Kowloon? A friend of someone I know works there. What will happen to her?"

"The news does not always report things accurately. Most employees will be reemployed." Gerard fingers his silkish tie. "That company is mismanaged and after being reorganized, it will be efficient and a good fit for us."

"Ooh, that's good to hear about getting her job back. But what do you mean about a good fit?" I tilt my head.

"Subsidiaries within a corporation are often diverse." He turns and makes sure Sofie is nearby.

"Can you explain a little more?" I ask.

"When your chefs prepare a particular type of cuisine, they do not include eight similar dishes. They prepare different ones to balance each other."

"Um, we don't have a chef, and my mom doesn't know how to cook, but I get it." What I don't get is if I can trust Gerard because I don't know him.

A black limo noses its way down the street, and a young guy gets out. He dashes up and whispers with

Gerard before running back. I stare 'cause he's the one who gave me the envelope at the Peak.

Gerard says, "I slipped away from my security detail. My intern reminds me I have another scheduled meeting."

He has an intern? Maybe someday I'll be one. Focus, Ellie, I tell myself. If he vanishes again, so will my chances of stopping the takeover.

I take a deep breath, ready to say what I've practiced a hundred times. "What's going to happen with Avabrand? The company is wonderful, but that doesn't mean you should take it over. My dad and his employees work hard and all have families." I grasp my headband as if it were a weapon. "Their work is kinda specialized, so they'll have to move to find other good jobs. Plus, my dad has to start a new company, if he can."

"That is an entirely different situation. It is a good firm." As he turns to say a few words to Sofie, his glasses turn inky black. Dad wears that kind of eyeglasses, too, that darken when the sun hits the lens.

"Exactly what different dish, er thing, does Avabrand have?"

"It is difficult to explain specific details." Gerard stares at me. "Unlike some of the board members, my brother is against the Black Turtle Group taking it over."

"So why are you going ahead with it?" I sound kinda demanding, so I'm glad lots of people are walking past me, sorta stuck in a corner.

"Perhaps my brother might change his mind to support me. If so, I am willing to vote on a business matter he desires."

"So if he votes with you to take over Avabrand, you'll give him the vote for another business matter?" Like Kipp telling me he'll scratch my back and I'll scratch his. Except that we're kids.

"Certainly. Now, about my brother—" Gerard's voice gets very low as he faces me with the sun on his back. He's no longer the emperor of a private corporation supposed to be worth gazillions.

"You mean Mr. Han?" I ask.

"My family name is also Han." Gerard's voice gets husky as if he remembered something horribly sad. "After my brother's arrival, he called me for a one-minute conversation indicating you wished to meet me. I did not know we would see each other at the YMCA."

"Sheesh. I'm sorry my flip-flop flew in the air and hit your leg. You see, I have skinny feet and flops only come in one width." No one will ever believe I'm explaining my shoe problem to a CEO.

He ignores the buzz of his cell text and checks on Sofie again, who's playing hide-and-go-seek behind the poles. One thing for sure—Gerard is a fussy babysitter.

His glasses are clear again, showing eyes that looked like mine when Mom said we had to move again. "Technically I have other means to get a certain percentage of votes from the board of directors."

Technically? He's starting to talk like Kipp. "Does that mean you'll still go ahead with taking over Avabrand?"

"Certainly. I do not welcome this interference. However, I will delay for a little while."

"Why are you telling me this?"

"I assumed you might know my brother's where-abouts, but you obviously do not. Otherwise, you would have mentioned it." He ends our talk and takes Sofie's hand.

I thought if I met Gerard, everything would be all right. I came all the way here, and I've failed.

I'll miss Kipp and Frankie parading down my street with her hot pink collar.

I'll miss Dad searching for his fattening cheese puffs Mom's hidden in our kitchen.

I'll miss softball with Cat in the spring when my favorite jacaranda trees are in bloom.

Everything I love—gone.

He's leaving because I don't have what he wants.

A window from the limo rolls down. The intern shoves his head and arms out of the window while pointing to his watch wildly and waving Gerard to get in. He picks up Sofie to walk toward the limo. She turns and waves to me.

When Dad taught me blackjack, he said I was lousy at figuring the odds.

Ms. Tang said Gerard loves gambling on risky things. Give him what he wants. Now.

I shout out, "Gerard, I'll make you a bet."

22

TURTLES CRAWL

He stops, walks back, and faces me again. "May I ask what you mean?"

"I can help you get together with your brother." He doesn't have to know I'm looking for Mr. Han again myself.

After a second, he replies, "If you must know, we had a disagreement several months ago. Except for the recent brief conversation, we have not spoken since."

"But —"

"It is unnecessary to talk to him in person. He can be overbearing when he dictates this and that matter."

Where have I heard those words before? *You were*

being bossy and saying I had to do this and that. Gerard is a little brother, like Kipp.

"But your brother wants to meet you. I saw him two days ago. We're buddies." I move out of the corner and breathe the air zipping through the harbor. "One more thing."

"Yes?"

"Mr. Han has a health condition."

Gerard almost drops Sofie and stays silent for a long while. "Are you certain?"

"He told me himself. It might kill him."

Why, why did I say this. It's a little lie. No, it's a big lie. Except it could be kinda true from what Mr. Han told me.

Gerard stares at me, his face pale, without saying a word. He puts Sofie down, and they run toward his limo and disappear.

I scream at myself in my head. So close.

Seconds later, a door opens and the intern runs out. "My boss wants to know if we can drop you off at some place in Central. It might rain any minute."

A limo ride? Boy, I want to. But not if I'm supposed to answer any questions in a car with Gerard. I lied to him. "Oh, uh, thanks, but my family's waiting for me over there, a few minutes away," I say and point to where the bookstore might be in the nearby skyscraper.

"No problem, if you're sure. By the way, my sister has those same color braces," the intern says, pointing to my silvery turquoise metal. He rushes back into the limo.

Wow—someone noticed my braces and didn't think they were funny-looking.

Kipp must be going nuts trying to stall Mom. And I really don't have time to think or analyze anything else. I scramble and trot away from the pier, trying to avoid pedestrians who come toward me at a crossroad before I turn off.

When I first walk into the bookstore, Mom and Kipp aren't anywhere, so I grab the book that I want to buy. As I'm paying for it, I ask the cashier if anyone left me a message.

"Oh, you must be Elizabeth. Your mother couldn't reach your cell and had to leave in a hurry," he says. "The little boy with her had some problems breathing. Here's a note for you."

Kipp sick? I hope and pray he's OK. Please hang in there, little brother. Mom's scribbled message says to get a cab back to the guesthouse ASAP.

I ask the cashier for directions to the nearest taxi stand away from the pier. But he's talking way too fast for me, especially when he explains a shortcut through the twin tower next door.

"Uh huh, uh huh." I'm not following anything.

"You can't miss it."

Groan.

On the footbridge, it's like seven million-plus people who live here surround me. In some ways they're all like family, except that they don't know me. I pull out my water bottle and take a long gulp and drain it. I pull myself together and exhale.

I can do this.

Off the footbridge, Mom's cell is useless. Not because it doesn't have GPS, but because I don't know where I'm going. My clothes stick to me like a damp, dirty dishrag soaked in sticky packing tape. I was hyped up a couple of minutes ago, but that was before I squinted up at 300-plus skyscrapers. You'd think this part of Central would be familiar by now.

Until an unusually tall building on the left and one on the right reminds me of Kipp's football goalposts. That's when he bragged about doing a pick-six, or whatever he called it. Using those as my landmark, I know I'm on one side of the Central downtown area.

I love landmarks.

Forget about a cab ride since most of my money

is gone. I walk down the street, dragging my legs, until I come almost face-to-face with dorky-looking mannequins wearing movie star clothing. Kipp and I saw those before, so that means the bus stop has got to be nearby.

Yup, here it is, and as I wait, a dreamy double-decker bus pulls up out of the blue. I march up the click-clacky steps. Once on, I'm not sure where I would get off 'cause I don't know the name of the main street near the guesthouse. And I haven't taken this type of bus before. I jump off before the doors slam shut.

I try calling the guesthouse to leave a message for Mom, but it goes to a voice mail. And it blips right away before I can even think of what to say. Screwed again.

Clueless. Moneyless. Phoneless. OK, a useless cell.

For some dumb reason, I remember Kipp's T-shirt that says, TO BE NO. 1, TRAIN LIKE YOU'RE NO. 2. I'll look for the subway, Kipp. I'll take it all the way to the guesthouse.

Fearless.

The clouds are about to burst wide open when I pass a subway entrance. The MTR symbol is exactly the way Kipp described it the first day we explored.

Inside the station, the wall map doesn't show a direct line to the guesthouse. Come to think of it, that's why we always got a ride or took a bus down to this area.

But I'm confused about which way I'm going. It's like the Peak Tram Illusion when Kipp and I were riding up with Mom. Except I'm not going up on the tram to Victoria Peak, and who knows which way things might fall.

I rummage through my backpack for my Octopus MTR card. If I don't have it on me, I don't know what I'd do with so little cash. As I'm about to strike out, I find the card in my back pocket. At last.

At last nothing—it's only Ms. Tang's business card.

People are buying tickets from a vending machine, so I line up behind a woman and see what she does. I copy her actions on where I want to go by pressing buttons on the screen map. After choosing one single-journey ticket, the price pops up.

All I have is my final ten-dollar note to put into the slot. Out comes my ticket. As I walk away, the person behind me calls out. I stop in my tracks.

She only motions I forgot my change. Lots of it—yay!

Afterward, I find my way to the Island Line that

has a stop at a university station nearest the guest-house. I'm OK when I get on, except for almost getting off at the first stop. I couldn't help it—I was standing near a crowd of people bunched up by the door.

A few minutes later when I finally get off the correct exit, all I remember from the map is a Pok Fu Lam Road that's supposed to be up here. I follow the crowd up many escalators and through scads of passages. On the street level, I ask people for directions, and they point to a steep walkway.

Riding the subway by myself and getting off in no time was the easy part. My tiredness level is now 20 out of 10. Buildings are on every level going up, and the guesthouse is supposed to be near the top. That means I'd have to climb the equivalent of several skyscrapers stacked on top of each other. With a sore toe. I'm not happy.

But it's not about me. I'm praying Kipp hasn't gotten worse.

My stomach's growling. When I dig deep into my backpack, I find a granola bar from my trip to the 7-Eleven with Cat. It's even got tiny chocolate chips—the junk fuel I need.

Except as soon as I take the first step up, zaa-zaa water pours out of the sky like a stuck faucet bursting open. At least it's not the highest-level typhoon I read about in the brochures. The other people are all hustling like it's going to get worse, though.

They were right.

Rain lashes out like silver spikes targeting the ground, and gusty winds don't care what's on their path. My umbrella turns into a satellite dish and blows away from me, twisting a few times, fluttering like a kite in trouble. I don't know where it ends up.

Kipp, I'm going to develop leg muscles—you wait and see. All your sports tips are helping us help Dad. And Mom, you bet I'll take your advice on how to be a better runner.

I love you, family. If sea turtles can crawl on land, I can climb outdoor stairways that go straight up. I concentrate by counting in Cantonese, and this helps me go up step by step. When I say *yat, yi, saam, sei, ng,* I can do five steps. And six to ten—*luk, cat, baat, gau, sap*—that's five more steps. Thank you, Ms. Tang, for that suggestion.

I breathe out to push myself and breathe in to quiet down. Exhaling gives me the burst of energy that Mom had stressed, and I know Dad would be proud of me.

Every time a walkway ends, I stop and ask for

directions and go around some buildings where another one appears. When I can't take it anymore, one more stairway means climbing again. Straight up.

A bannister appears out of nowhere, so I cry out and grab it to help me go up. Except that my hands are buttered ice cubes, and I can't get a good grip. As my hands slide off, I start tripping and almost lose my balance.

As the rain lets up, I start up again, slow as a turtle. I wish I knew how to count to one hundred in Cantonese. I could do it in Mandarin, but what if my pronunciation of the four tones is off? But who cares? Mom was right about me getting off the over-analytical boat.

Finally, when I make it to the very top, I recognize the quiet street in front of me. On the right, cars usually make a U-turn to get back on the main road. Like the first night when my family arrived and the cabbie threw out a weird phrase after he turned and passed me. Mr. Han explained the driver was only giving me a message. An ordinary message that freaked me out.

Things definitely aren't what they seem.

Turning left, I stumble toward the guesthouse.

23

UNDER YOUR NOSE

I STEP INSIDE and shuffle through a maze of hallways, holding my backpack in front of me and dropping it a few times. I'm about to sway on my floor when my family comes out with worried shouts and hugs me again and again.

"Ellie, I was so worried about you." Mom's eyes are all red and watery.

"El, you made it!" Kipp jumps up and down, so happy to see me he doesn't even look sick.

"Water, fast, please," I say in a raspy voice.

He unscrews one of the bottles by the doorway, where he placed them the night we arrived. And dumps the water right over my head.

I part my sopping wet hair, already damp, and say, "I meant to drink." I giggle like people do when they're sooo tired and see something sooo silly.

"Sor-ree, you gotta go with the flow. Here, I'll get you a towel."

"A clean one, please," says Mom as she gets me a glass of water.

I chug it down really fast and ask, "Kipp, are you feeling better?"

"Yup, it's only my pre-asthma that's kicking up." He glances at Mom and crosses his arms. He parks himself on the futon with his back turned like he doesn't want anyone to bother him. Except for Frankie if she were here.

Mom says to me, "After you left, I thought Kipp was having trouble breathing, but it was over soon. Still, it was a long 45 minutes since we left the book-store and arrived home."

"That's all? I must have left right afterward, but it took forever to get back. Your message scared the heck out of me." Someday I'll tell her I took a new subway line by myself. And describe those awful stairways I wasn't used to climbing.

"I'm proud of you. Did you have any problems picking up the ferry schedule at the pier?"

Yeah, it's all coming back. I lied big time to Gerard. It was more than what parents call stretching the truth. "I did get one, but now I'm exhausted. My head's a little woozy."

Mom sucks in her breath and says, "You didn't fall or bump your head anywhere, did you?"

"I don't think so, at least I don't remember."

Kipp rises from the futon and approaches me as if I'm wearing a "Fragile" sign. He says nice and slow like I'm an idiot, "A guy on my baseball team once had a concussion. Show me four fingers."

"You've got to be kidding." I raise three fingers about six inches from his face.

"Whatever. Wanna rest?"

"Hey, are you grading on the curve? You asked for four fingers."

"See, you're all better," he says.

We both rest—two sickies, kind of, who have one more day to save Dad's company.

Mom places a cold washcloth on my forehead before leaving to get food for me. While she's away, I tell Kipp as much as I know. "Gerard almost collapsed when I told him his brother has a medical problem. I'm guessing that deep down, they're close. Mr. Han does have high cholesterol, but he isn't anywhere close to dying. I kinda lied."

His eyes get big and round as if I got a triple and a run and also made a double play, all in one inning.

"Maybe you were pushed." He clutches his pillow and moves over while I sit down.

"And guess what? Can you believe I had to figure out cursive using Mom's Ankle Alphabet? Sheesh. Remember that T-shirt from the Stanley Market? It has a message—EBONY SEA ANIMAL CONNECTS ALL."

"What does all that mean?"

"In LA, Mr. Han said I was a black turtle. So I'll bet it means that I've got to bring the two brothers together. I think that's the key to stopping the takeovers," I say.

"If you don't talk again soon with Gerard, Dad's doomed."

"Don't I know it." I pause and ask, "I can see the next step but don't know how to reach it. What do you do when your team is down?"

"Oh, so you're dying for another sports tip? OK, I once asked my coach a dumb question about what I was doin' wrong." Kipp shakes his head. "First, he said there's no such thing as a dumb question, something dumb that all grown-ups say. Then he said it's not dumb to look for something right under your nose."

"Right under my nose. Hmmm, sounds dumb. When I talked with Mr. Han at the museum, he didn't say Gerard was his brother," I say. "I know he's absent-minded or he could have thought I already knew. He kept saying I had to find Gerard, and I'll have to try one more time."

"Those brothers don't know how to—what teachers say—communicate," says Kipp.

"Yeah, it's almost like Mr. Han is nervous to talk to his own brother. Sometimes when you and I fight, the parents step in. Could be that's what the turtle message on my T-shirt is saying." I get up and yawn. "Listen, after Mom returns, could you give me an assist with our plans for tomorrow?"

When she returns, she closes the bedroom door to talk to Dad on the phone. After I wolf down my food, I knock and poke my head in, waving my hand like a fast windshield wiper.

"The kids are all right . . . Good luck with that job interview, isn't it rush-rush? Also, when I return, I'll contact a real estate agent . . . Worse comes to worse, I could open a small catering business on the side . . . Ellie's getting to know her way around here. She traipsed all over the area today. Wait, here she is."

Job interview? Real estate agent? Catering business? This can't be for real.

I grab Mom's cell and go to the hallway outside. "Dad, what's this about an interview? Is it close to where we live? When do you go?"

"It's out of town, but it may not mean anything. I have to participate in multiple interviews to finalize a job offer." Dad's voice fades in and out.

"You promised not to sign any papers at Avabrand. You didn't, did you?" I ask.

"Well, I did sign—"

"WHAT?" I just about faint.

"But I haven't submitted them yet since I'm swamped," he says.

"You can still interview without sending off those final papers, can't you?"

He sounds pooped. "Change is hard, Ellie. I get it, but we've got to move on. Life has no guaranties."

"Dad, can you hold off—please," I beg.

"Listen, Sport, I've got to get going. Hopefully, you're keeping an eye on the Kippster and having fun."

Yeah, lots and lots of fun. But I don't want to worry him. "I love it here. So many things are different and yet, many are the same. One more thing, um, if someone tells sort of a lie to make a situation better, it's not a bad thing, right? Bye, Dad."

"Whoa, don't hang up—exactly what do you mean, young lady?" He sounds super alert.

"I'm kinda tired, but I have a friend who, uh,

meant to help another person. Now, she's not feeling good about it." It's always a friend.

"It's important that this person clarifies, or it might be hurtful. The person telling the lie will have to tell the truth."

"Of course, silly Dad. Love ya always."

"I miss you three so much. Love to Kipp." He hangs up when I can hear him fighting to keep his normal Dad voice.

I picture him eating a cold meal since the microwave often breaks down. He opens the freezer and deliberately picks ancient Spanish Rice leftovers for breakfast. That's cold crunchy rice with some Mom-type pasta sauce thrown on it. Someone's got to do the dirty work.

Dad's situation was miserable enough and then I had to lie to Gerard. Like how do I fix that now?

I return to the bedroom and ask Mom, "Did I hear you're going to contact a real estate agent?"

"That's right. If your dad finds another job, I'd rather have someone selected beforehand."

"But I can't move away from our house and neighborhood." I groan and cover my face with my hands.

"I know, but preparation is key for me." Discussion closed. Mom calls Kipp over. "Oh, I forgot to show you the Throwback Thursday pictures your dad sent before he called."

Two little kids, standing in front of the YMCA in our town. Kipp and I look at each other.

It's a sign to find Gerard and reunite him with his brother. There's only one place to go.

He gets the ball rolling. "Can we shop for new watches? El and I both need new ones."

"Again? It happens every few months. Why didn't you speak up at the Stanley Market?" Mom pouts while rolling her eyes. "It had lots of varieties that were also inexpensive."

"I got lost there, in case anyone cares. You're lucky to see me standing here now," says the little drama prince, waving his arms. "How about returning to the shopping area near the harbor on the Kowloon side? We know how to get there quickly."

Silence from Mom. She's making me nervous by opening her suitcase and packing early.

I jump in. "You know, I misplaced my journal, the one with all my notes for Dad. I think I dropped it at the Y, and that's near Kipp's shopping area. Plus, you could get in another good lap swim before our long flight home."

"I think I'll pass up circle swimming on the left

this time." Mom perks up and smiles at me. "Now about your lost journal—what you need is a nice, secure ziplock bag. A legend says it's a girl's best friend." She carefully slides one out of her deep pocket and hands it to me like she's serving tea to an empress of China. "Here's a spare for you in case your journal ever reappears."

If kids want to persuade a parent to do something, they can't roll their eyes. I'm stuck, so instead, I just about bow to her before gently accepting the bag.

"Mom, can you please, please say yes?" Kipp frowns and fidgets and freaks out—his three favorite f-words. "Gee, I sure miss Frankie," he says, pushing every button.

"What about *family*?" I'm so tired, I can barely say the word out loud.

Mom tells me to go to sleep as if nothing happened today.

Losing Kipp, meeting Gerard, and finding out Dad is already interviewing for a new job—everything's happened.

I conk out.

DAY FIVE

24

A PLACE YOU CAN GO

A RUNNER, a home-run wannabe, and a lacrosse trainee get off a subway exit in Kowloon.

The runner might change her mind, so we hotfoot it toward the YMCA.

The home-run wannabe hopes to reunite two brothers and save her dad's company.

The lacrosse trainee counts on giving the wannabe an assist.

Otherwise, he pretends to be the special face-off guy, something he learned on TV. (I won't snitch to Mom about the commercials.)

As we walk past the Peninsula Hotel, Kipp gives a thumbs-up to the line of Rolls-Royce cars and dim sum lunch.

I nudge his arm. "Wait, does that mean the same

thing here? Ms. Ohara warned my class some words or gestures we use might be a no-no in different places."

Mom says, "Ellie's right, be careful. Anyhow, let's not procrastinate. You're the one who wanted to go to the Y so badly." She walks ahead and suddenly stalls. "On second thought, let me pop into the Peninsula. I need to inquire about some of their desserts on the dining menus if they'll let me."

"For what?" asks Kipp.

"Excuse me?" I ask. Mom can't be serious about starting her own catering company. What she told Dad last night couldn't be for real. I picture an empty shop with no customers. No one. N.O. "Do you think that's a good idea? I mean, aren't we grounded?"

"Absolutely, so I'll watch you enter the Y from here. It's a good thing it's right next door, and you're only looking for your lost journal. No drama," she says. "Why don't you pick me up in half an hour on your way back? We'll buy those watches you two are so desperate to buy."

At the Y lobby, I tell Kipp, "Listen, this is our last day before leaving tomorrow. We've got to up our game to find Gerard, if by some miracle, he's here.

It's not so busy now, so hunting for my journal will be a good excuse to snoop around."

At the front reception desk, while Kipp looks on, I fill out a lost-item form.

Journal with creamy tannish paper, with a nice crinkly look. The first page has a stamped design that I don't know what it is. All the pages are glued inside a thin black leather case. The leather on the top has wavy edging. It's about 4x6 inches when closed. It's also wrapped around with a thin, black strap that isn't actually a rubber band but could be used as a hair tie in an emergency . . .

I continue describing it in different ways to make sure people know it's mine.

After about ten minutes, the staff member taps his fingers, but not like he wants more tea. "Excuse me, do you need more time? Your five-page report might be sufficient," he murmurs, while grasping the form out of my hands politely.

I thank him as Kipp and I leave. When the phone rings, he starts speaking in Cantonese, and sounds annoyed. "Oh, Miss," he calls out, putting up a hand. "Wait."

Kipp whips around and asks, "Who was that? What's happened?"

"She forgot her pen," he says while putting his

hand on the phone. He continues his call loudly in English, "No, I said we want the noodles in the beef soup, not stir-fried. Thank you. Mgoi saai." He says to us, "This takeaway place always mixes up my order."

"Don't you mean takeout?" I ask, reaching for my pen.

"That's my mom's favorite word," Kipp adds as he smacks his lips.

"That's what Americans say." The staff member smirks like we don't know right from left. "We say takeaway here."

"My bad. They sound similar. Anyhow, I'm sure your food will be yummy." I thank him as my cheeks get warm and warmer. What an idiot I am for trying to correct someone's English.

When we're outside the locker rooms, I ask Kipp, "Hey, could you zip in and look around? I'll wait right here—no matter what."

When he comes out and shakes his head, I'm not exactly surprised. "I'll check out the pool area. Let's meet in a few minutes back in the lobby. And don't get lost."

"The Vice President of Transportation doesn't get lost."

Well, except at the Stanley Market.

Hardly anyone is in the women's locker room, and when I peek in the leisure pool area, only a few kids are paddling around. No Sofie. No Gerard.

The world does not revolve around me.

On the way to the lobby, I take a corner too fast, like I'm on wheels, and stumble. English newspapers on a rickety stand scatter all over the floor. Great, just when I'm in a hurry. I thump my head with my hands.

As I pick up what's spilled, I glance at the news. One newspaper has a front-page sidebar of short blurbs about different companies.

I gasp when one of the blurbs screams out at me. It says, "Sources say the privately held Black Turtle Group will dismantle the California firm after the takeover. Although disagreements among board members have erupted, its CEO will complete details today." I scan the date that tells me it's an old edition.

No big deal, so I head toward the lobby again.

Five seconds later, I remember dates here rarely have the month-day-year order I'm used to. Like the sign in front of the closed Madame Tussauds wax museum at the Peak. Day, month, year—that's today's edition here. I return and reread the blurb.

O.M.G.

Gerard said yesterday he'd delay the takeover decision for a while. Wow, he couldn't wait. Instead, he had to get the board of directors together right away. They gave him the number of votes on the Avabrand takeover without his brother, Mr. Han.

And he'll run with it because the corporation's in control. It's got the sharpest swords on the right and doesn't care about families and what will happen to them.

I stand with my face down, shocked, and almost tear out my hair. I've come all the way for nothing. Like, why is this happening to me. I'm finished.

Unless the newspapers get things wrong. And I can do something about it.

I straighten myself up. I can go for it.

My family will not be kicked off our front porch.

I will stay in my school.

I will stay in my home.

Kipp will stay on his lacrosse team when he makes it.

Mom will stay with her job.

Dad will stay with his company.

Cat and my softball team and Coach Jen and Ms. Ohara and my neighbor Abbey's family and Kipp's friends will wait in my neighborhood. Even Russ. Hopefully.

I've got my loose headband as a sling.

I join Kipp and tell him what I discovered. "I need to give Gerard a message he and I have got to meet again. What do you think?"

"Remember, I ran into some shoppers at the Stanley Market when I was lost? You said we could visit that other hotel 'cause they were talking about swimmers," he says.

"Right—why don't we do a twofer at that Inter-Continental HK hotel tonight? You said it's near the Star Ferry Pier, right? I'll ask Gerard to meet me there as you distract Mom."

"I smell face-off! Wait, how are you going to contact him for the win?"

"I'll write a note," I say as we return to the reception desk. "If he's important, they'll forward the message to him somehow."

"Now you're talking. Time to put the pedal to the metal."

"Petal to the medal? Oh, that pedal—got it." I laugh and start writing.

Dear Mr. Gerard Han,

Remember me? I talked to you and Sofie yesterday when I finished my pretend flash mob dance. Could you please meet me at the InterContinental Hong Kong hotel between 7 to 8 p.m. tonight? It's the one practically next to the Star Ferry Pier. I want to tell you the truth about your brother.

Also, I'm leaving Hong Kong tomorrow.

Thank you,

Elizabeth Wei Pettit

P.S. If you see me with my mom, please pretend you don't know me.

With trembling hands, I get an envelope from the front desk and write out the only address I have.

To: Mr. Gerard Han, Black Turtle Group

Care of the Hong Kong YMCA in Kowloon

URGENT

The same guy who helped me file a report on my lost travel journal takes the envelope. Glancing down at the name, he kinda turns pale. He gapes at me but only says, "I will take care of this."

Kipp and I head back to the Peninsula Hotel to pick up Mom. I swing my arms as if I've got a bat in my hand. "I'm so glad I wrote that note. Ahh, the power of the pen."

"What's that got to do with baseball or softball?"

"Absolutely nothing," I say.

"You said the power of the pen. Like power of the bullpen, relief pitchers and stuff."

I giggle. "Sheesh. That's insane—people's minds don't work like yours."

"And what if Gerard sees us at the hotel together? Do you think he'll remember what happened at the Y?" Kipp fingers his rubber wristband.

"You mean the cannonball? His sketch pad did look half drowned."

"If I dye my hair, he won't know I'm related to you."

I tweak his hair. "I can't see you as a blond. Well, Dad's one, so anything's possible. You worry too much."

And I worry more.

25

WATCH AND WAIT

WHO WANTS to go shopping with Kipp again? That's crazy.

After we pick up Mom, he leads the way to nearby Nathan Road. I pick out a new watch within a minute. But little brother needs at least a week.

"Come on, Kipp, it's time to narrow down your choices. Pretend you get to choose the final four." Mom and I keep waiting for him to decide.

"So you're following college basketball playoffs now? I'm checking out the watches that glow in the dark. Don't rush me." He acts as if he's going to pitch a tent and stay a few more weeks in Hong Kong.

Wait—stupid, silly me. We need to hang around here longer, or we'll be at the hotel too early for Gerard. "Yeah, uh, take as long as you want. Did you see that wristwatch collection in the corner? Here, I'll help you decide."

After Kipp finally selects one and Mom pays the 400 HK dollars for both watches, I wince. Like can we afford little things like this in the future if she ends up as the only parent with a job.

Outside, Kipp squints at the sky and acts as if a cloud is ready to burst. "Um, Mom, can we go to this hotel near the pier and chill on our last night?"

"That's funny—if you think any moms can ever chill," she says, trying to get some kinks out of her neck. "Let's return to the guesthouse and pack."

Kipp looks at his new watch and stretches his neck to scan the sky again, kinda hyper. "Remember El said I could pick a place to visit? She said you said she's the boss on this trip. Come on, it won't take long."

Mom says she's getting dizzy following who said what until she nods after a minute.

He whisks Mom and me to the InterContinental a few blocks away, past the Star Ferry Pier. Gentle breezes wave softly as we go up the walkway and approach the hotel lobby. The hotel sits right on the water's edge.

"Kipp, do you think this is the place?" I whisper.

"Yup, this is it. I saw it on the same brochure you

were looking at," he says as we stroll in. "Maybe something will happen."

"You keep saying that. What's this all about?" He better not try anything too weird. But all he does is stick his nose up in the air and ignore me. Sheesh.

We luck out by grabbing lounge seats next to floor-to-ceiling windows showing off nighttime views. It literally takes my breath away. If I stretch my fingers out, I can almost touch the highways of light spilling from sleek buildings glowing against the dark water.

I'm going to miss it.

From where we sit, I can see boats heading to or from the Star Ferry Pier. "Let's take one of those ferries back to Central later," I suggest, pointing out the window.

"We'll see. Ahh, I didn't know this is the ultimate comfort." Mom hums and leans back against lounge cushions, perfect to cuddle up and take a nap.

Kipp asks, "What's up? You look totally happy."

"Can you believe it—I won a prize." A soft blush creeps up her cheeks. "Where, you ask? At a workshop in my hobby conference. I've learned how to make all kinds of desserts. All while you two play lazy tourists without a care in the world."

"Wow—what'd you make?" I ask, one of the lazy tourists.

"Chocolate cake. I don't mean to brag, but I got third prize. So wickedly delicious, it'll knock your softball out of the park."

"Third prize? You mean like one–two–three, the third digit when we count?" I hold up three fingers because I'm good at that. And I want to make sure she said *third* instead of *word* or *nerd*.

"That's right. Third prize in the BBC."

"The British Broadcasting Corporation?" My mouth drops open.

"No, the Beginner Bake-off Contest."

"Shut up—you rock." Kipp cheers, and we lean over and hug her. "Only, wait, we thought you hate to cook."

"Don't they teach you at school to be specific? I never said *bake* was a four-letter word, only *cook*. I wanted to make you a dessert you can sink your teeth into." Mom's eyelashes are getting wet as she blows her nose. "Don't tell your dad. I'll surprise him when we get home."

Dad. Now, wait a minute. He was the one who pointed out one important detail about Frankie's third prize in obedience class. The class only had three dogs. Like one–two–three.

Kipp and I stare at Mom with a big question mark.

I ask in a hushed voice, "By the way, uh, were many people in that baking contest?"

"About fifty or so. Why?"

"Way to go! You did it, you're cooking, I mean you're baking," I say as we give her high-fives. "Mom, one more thing—will you offer takeout, er, takeaway?"

She tilts her head, puzzled. "Whatever. Your shenanigans forced me to change my schedule so I could spend most of the day with you. So then I found a morning workshop I loved. Go figure—life is unpredictable."

That's for sure. I'm nervous as heck. What if Gerard receives my letter and rips it to shreds? And that means I'm wrong about him. Unless it's that guy over there if he turns around. Nope.

As I keep watching the crowd, a server presents us menus with a slight bow and ear-to-ear smile. She waits to take our order for lounge-seat dining. When I check out the prices, my brain says, "Leave here immediately and never come back."

Right away, Kipp takes out a wad of bills and gives it to Mom wordlessly. That includes my share of the HK dollars.

She chuckles while giving it back to him word-lessly, indicating it's her treat. "Buy something for Frankie." We scan the menu again that includes lots of food I'm familiar with.

I never knew I could order an All-American club sandwich here. When it arrives, I drown myself in crisp toast and just-the-way-I-like-it bacon. I don't say no to smoked turkey breast, tomato, and lettuce. I try a 'lil dab of mayo. Me, a mustard-lover, trying this in Hong Kong.

Eaters are leaders. Food gives us energy to get things done. I poke Kipp's arm and murmur, "Where the heck could Gerard be, if he even comes. We've got to stall."

About five minutes before 8 o'clock, Mom stands up and says, "Come on, let's go," she says. "I have a date to wash my hair."

The great staller spreads his arms on the back of the seats and sits back while fidgeting. "Um, Mom, aren't you too old to have a date? Hahaha. I mean, what's the rush? It's nice here."

"What an unforgettable skyline and the food is to die for, but I'm tired. Say bye-bye." She can hardly get her words out before covering her mouth to yawn.

More people cram into the lobby and eye our platinum seats since Mom's standing.

Where's Gerard? Him and me—we're the ones with an important date.

"Please, please, clouds, don't come any closer." Poor Kipp mutters to himself while looking at his watch and counting down.

"What's going on, Kipp?" I whisper to him. "What's out there? Tell me."

All at once, he explodes upward from his seat and points out the window. "Look, guys—put your hands together for this show!"

Lights instantly brighten up the clear, inky sky as if Fourth of July fireworks came out of nowhere. The waterfront skyscrapers of Hong Kong, so quiet up until now, light up with music and beam jet-like laser lights. They're all one-of-a-kind designs with their own rhythm but still in sync with the blaring music. I open my mouth, stunned.

Kipp acts like he's in math and sports heaven. "Hey, give it up. That one's got the kind of geometric designs in my book. See that building—it's got the lights they flash at night games when someone scores."

He and Mom can't keep their eyes away from the show. Same thing with the surrounding crowds who gaze at the zigzag lights from one side of the harbor to the other.

I'm still sitting at the end of our lounge seat and kicking myself. How useless was it to hand my message for Gerard to the YMCA reception guy.

I clap Kipp's shoulders. "The show is stunning—how did you plan all this?"

"You caught me looking up the info in the bathroom. At first I thought it was gonna rain, especially when those clouds came out. I wish Dad could have seen it."

"Me, too. Mom, is he still planning to interview for a new job? Please say no."

"I'm not sure and was hoping to talk to him again tonight. Whatever the situation, everything undergoes a process and takes time."

"Where's the place he's interviewing?" Kipp asks.

"It's odd, but he didn't have time to give details. Definitely not in California, though, is all he said." Mom cringes from my shocked face like the time I fell off my bike.

I take a deep breath. "Did he already send out those final, goodbye papers with Avabrand?"

"I'm unsure, but it's essential he gets a job before thinking about starting another company. They don't materialize that easily. Be right back."

She grabs her tote and says she'll be in the restroom.

"Kipp, Gerard's nowhere in sight. Can you hold off Mom if she returns early?" I get up and tug on my GOOD GIRLS STEAL softball wristband. At the front lobby door, I wait and wait and wait. No one greets me. N.O.

My wristwatch says it's about 8:30, later than the time on my note, so I turn to go. Why didn't he come?

"Hello, Elizabeth P.?"

I don't recognize that voice.

26

NIGHTTIME GLIMMERS

BUT I'VE SEEN her before. A woman dressed in an elegant business suit gives me a mom-type smile.

"Hello, I'm Rachel, pinch-hitting for my boss Gerard." She walks over and shakes my hand.

"Hi, uh, so he's not coming?" I ask.

"I am truly sorry, but I was in a meeting with him and am partly to blame. He's running late, so asked me to come first. He didn't want you to worry."

Oh? That's nice of him. So he did get my note. "Excuse me, didn't I see you by the YMCA pool when my flip-flops kinda ran into Gerard?"

Rachel laughs. "Yes, that was me. Think of it this way—you got his attention. By the way, I don't even know your last name."

"It's Pettit, but my middle name is Wei. It's my

mom's family name." I'm getting good at pronouncing it like *way*.

"Oh? Which character is it?"

I try to describe it for her and end up writing about eighteen strokes in the air with my finger. And I don't know the simplified version. I'm not that fast and have to pause a few times to take a breath or think about the next stroke.

Kipp runs up and says, "Mom says she'll be right back—still upset and looking for her ziplock thing. She's exhausted and wants to take the MTR back."

As if I have enough to worry about. "Rachel, this is my little brother Kipp," I say, glad to give my finger a rest.

"Nice to meet you. Weren't you at the YMCA pool, the one who did that—?"

He interrupts, "I saw lots of purses like yours at the airport stores and at the Peninsula shopping level. Aren't the views here great, and how did you meet my sister?"

I press my hand on his elbow and whisper, "TMI."

"I wear several hats. Officially I'm the Vice President of Transportation for the Black Turtle Group," she says and hands us business cards.

Kipp fingers the card over and over. "Wow, like me. That's sick."

I open, close, and open my mouth. "Uh, that's not what you think, Rachel. It means something different in America."

Her eyes twinkle as she says, "You don't have to explain—I have children."

We all laugh until a text pings from Rachel's purse. She ignores it while I pretend to talk to Kipp until he touches his nose. I grab his arm in case he starts a snot-basketball throw.

She finally reads her text and eyes me. "I'm more than sorry, Elizabeth, but an urgent matter came up at the last minute."

"Last minute? What do you mean?"

"Gerard can't make it at all. No one's sorrier than me to tell you this. No one."

All the way here and nothing to show for it on my last night here. My gut trembles like crazy as I force the ends of my mouth into a smile. "Thank you, anyhow, for letting me know."

No one's to blame. I glimpse past Rachel, pulled by the soft, glittering sights near the Star Ferry Pier. If I liked staying up late, this is where I'd want to hang out.

Night owls—Mr. Han told me he was one when

we talked in LA. As if he could be roaming by the Star Ferry Pier with its beautiful nighttime lights. Just a hunch.

But first, I'm sure he'd want me to fix something.

"Would you mind giving your boss a message?" I say, flicking back my head.

Rachel leans forward and peers at my face. "Are you all right?"

"Yes, please tell Gerard I lied about his brother's health. I might meet him soon if your boss can join us. You see, Mr. Han's a night owl," I blurt out.

Rachel looks confused. "Night owl? But of course, I'll deliver your message. I'm sure Gerard is tied up unexpectedly." She gets another text and waves goodbye to leave. "I must run along, too, as I have a date with my family. I'm so glad we met and wish you the very best."

Kipp says, "So many moms with dates tonight. What now, boss?"

"Freaking T-shirts—we've got to focus. Gerard's going to take over Avabrand if I can't close the deal. Who knows if he'll believe my message from Rachel?" All I want is to go outside to shriek and howl.

Mom catches up to us. "We need to get home the

fastest way possible. I want to catch your dad before he leaves for work."

"Could I talk with him, too?" I ask. If he handed in those final papers, we're all screwed.

"It'll be touch and go as he's going to the office briefly and afterward, straight to the airport."

"You mean he's got that interview like today? Guys, hurry, let's make the next Star Ferry," I say.

"The subway please, dear daughter, whose diapers I happily changed 24/7 when you were a baby. I'm ready to drop."

"But, the ferry's right here, and it's our last chance to ride it before we leave tomorrow."

Kipp butts in. "Yeah, and who wants to get all sweaty walking underground on the MTR? How about you and me, Mom, do rock-paper-scissors?" He sticks his hand out invitingly, and one person wins after his challenge.

That's what I call the assist of the year. He deserves a medal. Or a new cell. Wait—maybe not that, yet.

"I'm in," says Mom, with a glum look, and leads the way out.

"I'm pooped," says Kipp. "Don't wanna be Vice President of Transportation anymore."

"I'm shocked. I thought you like competition." Who can understand little brothers?

As we approach the Star Ferry Pier, a tour guide speaks loudly above the noise. "Victoria Harbour, named after the British sovereign Queen Victoria, is one of the most stunning places in the world. Crossing the harbor on the Star Ferry, opened in 1888, costs about 50 cents in US dollars. It's the best way to see the magnificent views."

I know that. TMI. We're leaving tomorrow, and I do not want to stand here listening to the wonders of Hong Kong I'll think about for a long time.

"By the way, the historic cross-harbor swim from Kowloon to Hong Kong resumed after thirty years." The tour guide continues blabbing. "How thrilling to see swimmers racing across the harbor doing front crawls during this spectacular annual event."

I didn't know that—swimmers?

I rush past Kipp and stumble, hitting my sore toe again. While hopping on one foot, I ask the tour guide. "Excuse me, sir, I'm not part of your group. But can you tell me about when the harbor swim contest first started?"

He checks his notes on a clipboard. "No worries. I believe it was over a hundred years ago. Ah, here it is, in 1906."

"Thank you." I gulp, glimpse Mom ahead of us, and turn to Kipp. "This is the place—Victoria Harbour with its amazing views at night. And swimmers doing the front crawl over a hundred years."

Seek a place of long-ago wonder
vessels by the sea
fast crawls, British name
gentle breezes, sovereignty
Since baak nin
alive with swimmers
glittering sights and
nighttime glimmers

How many times did we mention Victoria Harbour, the one with the funny *u* that's silent. I never thought about swimmers here 'cause my mind zeroed in on what's obvious.

Mr. Han jotted down where he thought he would be all right. In his own way.

He's got to be close by in this area. I don't have the most perfect info, but I've got to make do with what I've got. Maybe he's on one of these star ferries since that's a boat or vessel by the sea. But I'd still have to find Gerard. Again. And tell him that Mr. Han isn't sick and dying.

Even if the Black Turtle Group takes over Avabrand, I can still get the brothers together.

As Mom buys tickets for the ferry, I ask to use her cell. She says, "Fine, but please make it quick if it's that important." She kinda watches me.

Pulling out Rachel's card, I text her using as few letters as possible. "NO on ferry."

I'm sure she'll remember Mr. Han is a night owl. So I give myself a pat on the back for sending off my message. Wait. Or, could she think I wrote, "No one's on ferry."

I tell Kipp, and he jumps up and down and waves his arms like spectators in a close game. "No, no! She doesn't know you're a word nerd—enthusiast, whatever. It's one of your silly palindromes. She'll think you wrote *noon*."

Freaking T-shirts. Gerard can't show up at the noon ferry tomorrow. I'll be on a plane to California. All I can do is hit the ground running down the ramp to board the ferry, flying past Kipp and Mom. People in front of me look up, startled, and open up a path. One person mumbles about crazy speeders and shakes his head.

As I reach the end of the boarding ramp, the crew puts up the passenger barricade.

"But, sir, I don't think that boat is full," I say, out

of breath, as they ignore me. After all, I'm not part of the crew, so I plod back to join my family.

Waiting is hard. Like counting down the days and minutes and seconds until my birthday. Mom organizes her plastic bag of bags in her tote. Kipp passes the time by pretending to shoot imaginary balls into a lacrosse net. Me? I'm in a funk and don't want to talk.

In a few minutes, the next ferry arrives for us to board.

I scour the passenger area on the main deck. No one. Silly me to think Mr. Han would be on this ferry. All I can think about are the changes waiting for my family at home. To calm myself down, I focus on the tiny, gentle waves slapping against the boat.

Mom keeps getting up and changing seats.

"We've over here," I shout out.

Uh-oh. She comes up to Kipp and me with a greenish face like she's begging for a barf bag. "Kids, I mean guys, did I ever tell you I get seasick on boats? I thank my lucky stars the world has other modes of transportation now. Let's get off."

27

GET ON THE BOAT

KIPP JUMPS up and takes her arm. "Breathe deeply. Remember, you're a wonderful mom with kids— smooth sailing."

Mom kinda chokes. "Uh, let's not go there. Didn't you know how I feel about boats?"

I try my best to speak in a relaxing tone while glancing around. "The ferry goes straight to Central. How about grabbing those seats farther up that will catch a good breeze? Up near the woman wearing a bright blue top."

Mom peers at where I'm pointing. "That should help. But, of course, you mean green top."

"You're right," I say, even though she's wrong. I'll have to thank Ms. Blue Top someday.

Kipp stays with her while she sits and takes deep breaths, facing the water.

As the ferry is about to cruise out, it gives a little lurch and slides back and stops. On the pier, flashing lights and screeching cars come to a stop. It's dark, and with all the commotion, who knows what the heck is going on. Men who act like security guards race down the ramp. When I stand up to look, they've disappeared. Maybe a movie star came on board. Or, the queen of England.

Kipp comes back to me and asks, "How come the ferry was able to backtrack a little?"

"Maybe a vice president of transportation like Rachel yelled out STOP," I say.

"I want my job back." He scans his glow-in-the-dark wristwatch and reports about ten minutes or so before we dock.

Talk about pressure—like hoping new cleats will earn me a home run. "Can you wait here for a sec?"

I tell myself to think happy thoughts before checking out the ferry. Near the back, away from the seating area, is an odd little nook. A narrow staircase, almost hidden, stands in a corner.

I'm not afraid.

I return and point to the area and tell him about

the staircase. "Kipp, pssst, could you return and sit with Mom? I'm going to explore up there."

"What's up there? A bathroom?"

"I hope not. Later, bro."

"OK, boss. You've got this."

I was an idiot for telling Kipp at the airport we wouldn't talk sports in Hong Kong, ever.

Face-off. Making shots on goal. Playing behind the net. That's me.

Running back to the little nook, I take a deep breath and lean my head against the wall by boat crew jackets hanging on a rack. And bump into another jacket. Right under my nose.

I've seen this jacket before. I know the person wearing this jacket doesn't like heavy rain, what we have in common. I trip up the staircase, making as much noise as I can.

The ferry pulls out again.

In a cramped room with lots of instruments and controls, a skipper is at the steering wheel. He wears a baseball cap with a nautical symbol and a polo shirt with a cricket design. I'm on to him for his sports clothing.

"Hello?" I whisper. "Mr. Han, tell me it's you again."

"Ah, Elizabeth P., come on in. A little crowded,

but this is what they call the wheelhouse, or the pilot's room of the Star Ferry," he says, eyes crinkling, as he hands the wheel to another skipper. "I started volunteering here in the evenings. I see you kept your head above water."

"Barely. Is your cholesterol thing getting better?"

"Unfortunately, it runs in my family. I often get side effects from medicine, so I'll work harder on cardio exercises like lap swimming." He sighs. "Early this year, an uncle passed away from a heart attack, and my brother was especially heartbroken."

"I'm very sorry. Um, so your brother is Gerard, the CEO of the Black Turtle Group. And you're the chairperson of the board?"

Mr. Han nods. "Didn't I tell you? My position is no longer minute-to-minute work. I'm getting older and want to be challenged in different ways. Gerard manages the businesses." He pauses. "However, I still want to keep an eye on my little brother."

"I know exactly what you mean. By the way, why aren't you two talking?"

"Well, he's still upset with me about a business deal. I eventually took the fall for him without him knowing. Can you keep that between us?" His eyes twinkle.

"I'll zip my lips. I've taken the blame for my brother, too," I say. "But—"

"When we met in LA, it shocked me to hear about your dad's company. With no facts, I couldn't say anything. Even when we met at the museum, I was in the dark."

"Me, too, and it was hard figuring out how you acted in class to understand your notes. I kinda took a chance by bluffing the two of you could meet." I wipe my eyes flooding with tears and groan. "Now you're here, and he's nowhere."

Mr. Han says, gentle as a slight breeze in the harbor, "Don't worry about it. I spoke briefly with Gerard when I arrived and mentioned you. We have certain, ahem, communication issues. Taking over Avabrand isn't in the best interests of the Black Turtle Group."

"Huh? You mean it was all a ridiculous mistake?"

"Ah, Elizabeth P., it's not that simple. When our firm started out, a rival stole some designs and almost wiped us out. That was after our families had invested money in us. Gerard never forgot our uncle's family barely had enough food on the table." Mr. Han shakes his head. "In fact, he still gets hotheaded seeing similar designs, even from small companies."

"Wait—are you saying he thinks my dad stole his work? That's what the news hinted at."

"Gerard might think that after seeing Avabrand's small sea animal designs. Sometimes, similar ideas are hatched by people or companies in different parts of the world," explains Mr. Han. "The trick is to figure out if it's deliberate."

"Dad would never in a gazillion years steal someone else's designs, so why would Gerard even think that?" I stare at him, kinda tense, and clutch the straps of my backpack.

"He's protecting his turf. Occasionally, he does it in a crazy different or crazy emotional way. But he's a great brother and I love him."

Someone coughs.

We both jerk our heads up. Two people walk in holding hands.

"Oh, hey Gerard," says Mr. Han.

"We are pleased to see where Uncle Walter hides out as a volunteer," his brother says, wearing a casual polo shirt.

Sofie grabs her uncle's arms, and she and I give each other a little wave.

The two brothers hug like they haven't seen each other in over a century. They whisper about Mr.

Han's health, while Gerard looks up and down at him.

I blurt out, "I didn't mean to lie and say your brother is very ill—I'm sorry."

Mr. Han chuckles. "No worries—I explained. Oh, Gerard, have you formally met Elizabeth P.? She was a student in my Los Angeles class."

"Actually, my name is Elizabeth Wei Pettit," I say loud and clear.

"Wei—like the ancient kingdom?" asks Gerard.

"Yes, that's the one. Um, I never expected to see you again."

"I received a tip from my colleague, Rachel. Upon arriving, a boy on the main deck almost pushed us up the stairs. He is too young to be a tour guide, but he carried a clipboard like I did as a child. Those kids always know what they're doing."

"That's my brother. He's like a relief pitcher, always looking out for me."

"Little brother?" Gerard looks at me closely. "I believe I saw him previously at the YMCA."

I gulp and say, "That's right. I hope your sketch pad didn't get too splashed." I'm lucky that Sofie tugs her dad's arm and whispers to him.

"My daughter especially likes the toy you gave her. May I ask where you purchased it?"

"My mom's friend, Ms. Tang, gave me that sample. Her company makes creative toys here. Wait, I still have her card." I fish it out and hand it to Gerard.

"Oh? We will give her a call. Thank you."

Mr. Han says, "Tang? I assume she's the one who left me a message about your whereabouts yesterday. What a miracle I reached you at the Stanley Market."

"The T-shirt with with that puzzling design? I used my mom's crazy method to figure out the cursive."

"Sometimes luck gets a push," says Mr. Han, smiling.

I face Gerard. "When I first talked to you at the Y, I was sort of scared. Do you remember?"

"I do not recall, but I remember you are quite athletic," he says.

"Me?"

"When Sofie dropped her pool toy, you swam over as if you were being attacked by sharks. You frightened my intern when you raced after him at the Peak, Elizabeth."

"Oh, that—I mean, it's not as if I was doing the cross-harbor swim or anything. And please call me Ellie."

"You must be a good base runner, too," says Mr. Han, getting carried away.

I pretend to pull back my hair when I'm really yanking my locks.

Close the deal.

"Is the Black Turtle Group going to take over my dad's company?" I ask.

28

IN TIME

THE HAN BROTHERS ARE SILENT.

"Technically, yes," says Gerard. "However, the decision has not been completed yet."

No way. Please tell me, no way. I can't go back home with any *yet* talk.

Mr. Han says to him, "She is certain her father did not imitate any of your work."

No response from Gerard.

"Ah, Elizabeth P., why don't we do this?" Mr. Han gives me a warm, familiar gaze. "Do you maybe have evidence to show your dad's designs are probably his own creations?"

Coach Jen said batters must close the deal by running the bases if they hit the ball. *Maybe* doesn't count. *Probably* doesn't count.

"I–I don't think so. My dad uploads sketches to his company website, so I wouldn't have access to it." I stare down at my sneakers, wondering what more I can do.

The three of us don't say a word. I pinch myself while glancing outside at yellow flotation rings hanging by the window. As if they could save me.

Focus, Ellie, focus. When I brush my teeth too hard with my right hand, Mom tells me to use my left hand. Dad once told me if nothing turns out right, think about turning left.

In a low voice, Mr. Han says, "One of your homework mentioned you always carry keepsake items about your family. I remember that assignment on my desk after you left."

"Did you say *left*?" I leap up and yank my backpack off my shoulders. Plunge my hand to the bottom. Grab my family memories box. Rip open the clasp. Paw through the contents.

I hold up Mom's three-sentence recipe for Spanish Rice on an index card. Nope.

I toss a photo of Kipp wearing a dorky hockey helmet back in the box. Nope.

I laugh at Dad's sketch during a movie about a guinea pig in a flash mob dance. Nope.

I fumble for a tissue. "I don't have anything—this is just an old drawing of his."

"Excuse me, that sketch is interesting. Is that a guinea pig?" Gerard asks sharply. He picks it up and smiles with a dreamy face Dad also has when he looks at drawings. "Can you kindly recall when your father drew that?"

"I'm not sure. Wait, he always pencils in a date somewhere—here it is, about five years ago."

"I sketched a similar design, I believe, a few years later. May I kindly take a look?"

I blow softly on the drawing, hoping for some magic, and hand it over. As he reaches for it, my fingers brush against his heavy, gold cuff links. I adjust my headband, pretending I have a sword at my side like the knights in Mom's story.

Gerard looks at the design. Every line. Every stroke. Every curve. Like staring at the gazillion look-alike tiles in my bathroom and picking out the one that doesn't belong.

He holds the drawing up to the light like he's checking for water marks. "Do you still have that swim satchel with your father's design on the outside?"

I rummage through my backpack again and

hand my sackpack to him after taking out my damp swimsuit.

I follow Gerard's eyes. "Uh, my dad says once in a while he sees something, and years later it'll pop up when he's sketching." Sheesh. Did I hurt Dad? "I mean, before you did your sketches of course. Heh-heh."

"I have similar experiences," Gerard says, glancing at me and returning to the sketch.

Minutes pass. Or hours. My swimsuit must be dry. Waiting is like hoping my tiny zits will disappear before school starts.

That's when Gerard touches his brow and says, "We launched a set of tiny sea animal designs a few years ago. I was skeptical when Avabrand's work, very similar to ours, came on the market early this year."

"Do you notice anything?" I ask, swallowing hard.

"Your dad's older sea animal sketch is like the design on your swim satchel. This is his Avabrand work. He did not steal my designs after all."

I want to melt in a pool of the most heavenly ever chocolate.

Gerard and Mr. Han talk quietly together. They're speaking Mandarin Chinese, but it's too fast for me and I don't recognize most of the vocabulary. I wish.

"Does this mean everything's OK now?" I ask, hugging my backpack.

Gerard makes a phone call, frowning slightly, while Mr. Han tries to be cheerful. "Don't worry."

Not again.

Finally, Gerard gets off the phone and has another whispered conversation with Mr. Han who turns to me. "Ellie, may I keep your dad's original sketch for a while to show the attorneys? I'll mail it back to you."

"Sure! But, is my dad's job and his company safe? Like guaranteed?"

"Absolutely," say the Han brothers.

"Thank you, thank you so much. And it was so nice meeting both of you." I give them the home run of all smiles.

Sofie's dad pats her head while saying to me, "I appreciate your help to connect with my brother again. Life is unpredictable."

"And that's a good thing. Gerard, have your intern call my intern to get together." Mr. Han chuckles and pauses, holding up his hand. "Better yet, here's my new cell number. Call anytime."

Little brothers are worth having around.

I was wrong about important people in business. They don't always wear suits and carry laptops. One has a daughter. Not in a dark room facing me, but on the most amazing ferry crossing Victoria Harbour.

I say to Gerard, "If you ever visit Los Angeles, I could help you out."

He grins, showing an honest-to-goodness Kipp-like dimple. "May I ask in what?"

"I started watching kids if Sofie ever needs a sitter. You know, in case you're in a meeting." We smile at each other—the Babysitters Club.

I hug Sofie before she and her dad take off. But suddenly, he makes a U-turn and returns.

Uh-oh, Dad once said life has no guaranties.

"Oh, I almost forgot." Gerard takes something out of his jacket pocket and hands it to me.

"My travel journal! Oh, thank you," I say, taking it. "How did you—?"

"A person at the Y reception desk asked me to forward this if we met again. He said you wrote the most detailed lost-item report in the YMCA's history."

That's a hundred-plus years. I've made waves. Mom would be proud as I carefully place it in my inherited ziplock bag, safe from any international funny business.

I open the page marked by a sticky note listing the reasons behind a company takeover. Yeah right. Things aren't what they seem. I know that now.

After Gerard and his daughter leave, Mr. Han asks, "Is this all you hoped for?"

"It's so much more. You were right—things happened once I committed to helping Dad." I'm feeling like Frankie when she wags her tail.

"Ah, Elizabeth Wei Pettit, I'm proud of you for figuring things out, especially since I myself was in the dark. You believed."

"But I had lots of help. You nudged me first. I had Kipp and Mom. I thought about things that Dad, my softball coach, my English teacher, and my bestie said to me. Even my next-door neighbor and her two little boys. They were all with me at different times."

"By the way, you mentioned you're the guinea pig for outside classes. Can you recommend others who may be interested in the heritage class next spring? I might include sports played during a few Chinese dynasties." He flashes his best recruitment smile.

"I might know someone. It'd be cool if you could include what athletes wore back then. Certain kids, uh, think uniforms are the best part of sports." I see our ferry approaching the pier on the Central side. "Anyhow, I hope to see you again."

"Right, you never know."

I wave goodbye and leave. Oops, I return.

"I forgot—this is for you." I dig into my backpack one more time and hand him a manual I bought at the bookstore.

Scratching his head, Mr. Han devours the latest edition of *Little Brothers for Dummies* like a starved man at an all-you-can eat buffet. He never looks up when I leave again.

Ebony sea animal connects all. I'm a black turtle, and I did it.

I fly down the narrow staircase and find my family near the exit ramp. Kipp and Mom don't act worried. I mean where could I go and what could I do on one itty-bitty boat?

"El, did everything come out OK in the bathroom or whatever was up there?" asks Kipp, in a brotherly way.

I pull my family to me and say, "Group hug."

Kipp breaks away first, explaining that group hugs are done when a sports dynasty wins a championship. Like Mr. Han said, that's crazy—crazy good or crazy emotional. But, most of the time, Kipp's a great brother, and I love him.

"Mom, how do you feel?" I ask.

"Much better—maybe my sailing days aren't over." She tosses her head and grins.

"Wait, I thought of something," I tell her.

"What's that?"

"You always told me to get off the OA boat since I'm overanalytical. But when I do, I'm left with two letters—BT—in the word *boat*.

"And?"

"Nothing, nothing. Just a coincidence that a lazy kid tourist would come up with. So long, Victoria Harbour and the Star Ferry." We're the last ones to leave.

When I found out the world is bigger than my family and me, I didn't know I'd literally be running around in a new place far from home. Trying to solve a mystery based on understanding people got me pooped. When I first came off the plane in Hong Kong, I was so confused and scared.

My butt doesn't hurt now.

DAY SIX-SEVEN

29

WEI TO GO!

KIPP CARRIES his ratty umbrella all the way to the airport and then trashes it at the terminal. "Hey El, you delivered in the clutch."

"Yup, we both did. But it was touch and go for a while." I put down my book, bought with leftover money at the gift shop.

"How about getting a head start on your thank-you note," suggests Mom, a time management parent. Our vacation's over, and she's bossing me around to do routine stuff again. "When we're home, you can pop it in the mail to Betty."

Another interruption. I sigh and stop reading about the Yellow River in northern China—now, that's a lot of water. "Betty?"

"Sorry, Betty Tang. Ms. Tang to you."

"Seriously, the initials BT? Isn't her real name Elizabeth? I think that was on her business card."

"That's right, but I've always known her as Betty." Mom pulls out a deluxe slider bag and pulls out fancy thank-you cards she carries on trips.

"One more thing. Why did Ms. Tang say she and I have something in common? Is it our names?" I take the note card and fish out my pen.

"She did? Hmm, well, she was an English major and loves words and reading as you do. Oh wait, she had a brother near her age. She said they always did wacky things together. Sound familiar?"

Dear Ms. Tang,

It was so nice meeting you. Thank you for treating my family to delicious dim sum. After you taught me how to count to 10 in Cantonese, I found it useful going up lots of steps. I also want to thank you for contacting my teacher, Mr. Han. In the end, everything came out OK. Really OK.

XOXO,

Elizabeth Wei Pettit

P.S. Your toys are so creative. I hope you get lots more business.

After zonking out on the plane practically the whole flight, we arrive back in Los Angeles when tomorrow is today. Dad drives up with Frankie Wei and rushes out of the car.

Little brother hugs Dad and gets in. "Come here, girl, love you. Who's a good girl? Were you a good girl? Were you? Yeah, come here, you."

I give Frankie my gift, a rubber ball made mostly from rice husks and bamboo. It's not a bribe, but I'm hoping this will be the beginning of a beautiful friendship.

Kipp comes out of the car. "Dad, I missed you—guess what? I behaved and kept my clothes clean. And I didn't talk about sports all day." His dimples are working overtime.

Dad hugs him before planting a kiss on Mom's nose—sort of gross but totally adorbs. "It's funny. I had a positive job interview on my recent trip. However, early this morning I received an extraordinary email that Avabrand won't be taken over."

We squeal and jump up and down. Kipp pumps his fist in the air, and Mom takes out her tissues for whenever she pretends to have allergies. She settles in her usual seat, riding shotgun.

Dad wraps his arm around my shoulder before I get in the car. "Hey, Sport, what'd you do, where'd you go, what'd you see?"

I blurt out, "I missed you so much. It was incredible visiting all these places and we had one pair of goggles at the YMCA and Kipp got these allergies, I mean pre-allergy attack. I found out things I never knew about Mom and saw the coolest museum and fell in love with the Star Ferry." I bury my head on his chest.

I don't tell him about all the running here, there, and nowhere when I didn't know how or when or the way to do things. And all the hours ticking by. Thoughts of Dad packing up his office, thoughts of us moving, and Mom crying about the health insurance.

He tells me we can talk some more later and tweaks my hair and headband. I have lots to tell him, but not everything. A kid never wants to scare her parents.

At home, I jump out and call Cat who promises to pick me up tomorrow before our game.

Mom says she'll grill some hot dogs for anyone who comes home with us afterward. She swears she can't mess that up—and that she'll have a surprise dessert.

That night, I wait until dark and sneak into the kitchen. I tear off the "Eat at Your Own Risk" sign an anonymous kid put up on the fridge. Mom's fridge.

That's so yesterday.

————

THE NEXT AFTERNOON I peek out at the patio where Kipp is wiping sweat off his forehead.

His friend Wynnie unwraps a gift wrapped in clean toilet paper. He tells her the paper is recyclable, and she giggles like it's the funniest thing. She plays with the click-clacky beads on the thin vertical wires of her gift. "Oh, wow, an abacus. I love these beads! You'll have to teach me how to do these math calculations. Thanks, Kipp."

Kipp hands her a book about abacuses. "This is from the bookstore where I got sick." He says it slowly and clearly like it's rehearsed. You see, Mom corrected him after he told Dad, "A bookstore in Hong Kong made me sick."

First he was a toddler, next he learned the alphabet, but not in cursive. Today, he shows off how to use an abacus to his *GF* classmate. And no, Wynnie's not his girlfriend, at least not now.

It turns out she has to eat gluten-free food.

Kipp didn't let me down. He gave me an assist so many times.

When Cat stops by with her softball glove, I give her my gift.

She says, "Ellie, oh, I love this little sampan. Now tell me everything."

We head toward the park with our bats and gloves, and I pour it all out. How I overanalyzed things left and right and was scared of failing and got lost and found Kipp and how his sports advice helped me bring Mr. Han and Gerard together. And how I was in a place with mostly Chinese people.

"You know, Cat, it's fun being a Wei and a Pettit." I never thought I'd say that.

At the game, Kipp wears a T-shirt that says I RUN LIKE MY SISTER. TRY TO KEEP UP. He marked up a stinking undershirt with a marker, but I'm not complaining. Frankie's with him, chewing on her new ball like she's in Hong Kong heaven.

He yells, "You're killing it, El!" The inning hasn't even started—whatever—but I give him a thumbs-up from the dugout anyway.

Wynnie joins him, too, along with Abbey and her two sons who are walking up. Even Russ shows up. (Finally, I can focus on him! Maybe I'll see him after the game—I'm betting he likes desserts.) They all start the wave in the first inning. It ends at the third bleacher, but we only have one–two–three bleachers.

During the bottom of the final inning, the two teams are tied. I'm the next batter.

The ball comes toward me, spinning and hurtling, and I'm ready. I swing and get a pop fly but, lucky me, it's fouled.

I end up getting a walk and as the pitcher throws to Cat, the next batter, I steal the next base. I wasn't even thinking about it. I did it. When the catcher throws wildly to second, the ball heads to the outfield. I sprint to home plate.

I went and got my run. Not a home run, but a perfect, A-OK run.

After the game, Cat says to me, "Wei to go!" She hands me a new wristband that each teammate gets after scoring a first run. My fingers rub over the words I love before I pull it over my hand.

Home is the best place.

letters handed down in her family? Or will the lady's secrets in a Rome art gallery remain undeciphered?

It's up to Cat to solve the riddle.

If only five hundred years didn't stand in her way.

ACKNOWLEDGMENTS

I couldn't have written this story without all the teachers and librarians who recommended titles and encouraged me to always have a book in my hands.

Thank you to the always enthusiastic Callie Metler who believed in my book.

I am so appreciative of Esther Hershenhorn's guidance through the big-picture ideas. She shared with me all the themes and issues of my book and became my biggest cheerleader.

A very special thank-you to my friend Lynn Downey for her lyrical comments during our online writing course. After her first feedback, I knew I'd want to stay in touch. I'm so grateful to her for reading my initial manuscript and giving me valuable feedback.

How can I ever thank my amazing writing friends, Sherri Ashburner and Shirin Shamsi, for their detailed assistance and encouragement? They read, recommended, and reread final versions multiple times. I could not be a writer without their wisdom and support.

Thank you so much to my critique groups, both in-person and online, for reading my chapters and providing critical input on plot and character. They gave me needed advice to overhaul my manuscript when I thought I was done. More importantly, they answered all my questions and told me to keep going.

Special thanks to the Society of Children's Book Writers and Illustrators for their many workshops and conferences. They are a resource heaven for new writers.

I want to thank my family from the bottom of my heart for their support. My journey wouldn't be possible without their helping hands.

ABOUT THE AUTHOR

LEE Y. MIAO grew up in a small Pennsylvania town with a library to die for. Before writing K–12 educational materials and middle-grade fiction, she worked in the financial industry. Lee lives in New York with her family and a tireless dog.